LINE IN THE DUST

Isaac looked at the cowboys gathered in a circle. He saw reproach in the eyes of many. Word had gotten around, and they were siding with Runyan.

Isaac knew he had spoken harshly and out of turn. But it had been building in him, and he had said it, and now he wouldn't take it back for two hundred dollars. He chewed his lip and cast about for an argument that would hold water.

"Whatever trouble me and Pete Runyan have got, *I'm* man enough to put it aside till we get this job over with."

Runyan shrugged. "I reckon I can set it on the shelf too, till we've got this thing done for the Major."

Joe Sample studied both men critically, and with anger. "What *then*? You goin' to kill one another?"

No answer came from either man. . . .

Bantam Books by Elmer Kelton

THE DAY THE COWBOYS QUIT
HONOR AT DAYBREAK
THE MAN WHO RODE MIDNIGHT
THE TIME IT NEVER RAINED
SLAUGHTER
THE FAR CANYON
THE GOOD OLD BOYS
MANHUNTERS
WAGONTONGUE

WAGONTONGUE

Elmer Kelton

BANTAM BOOKS
NEW YORK TORONTO LONDON SYDNEY AUCKLAND

WAGONTONGUE

A Bantam Domain Book

PUBLISHING HISTORY

Ballantine edition / August 1972
Bantam edition / September 1996

DOMAIN and the portrayal of a boxed "d" are trademarks of Bantam Books,
a division of Bantam Doubleday Dell Publishing Group, Inc.

ISBN 0-553-27467-8

Published simultaneously in the United States and Canada

Bantam Books are published by Bantam Books, a division of Bantam Doubleday Dell Publishing Group, Inc. Its trademark, consisting of the words "Bantam Books" and the portrayal of a rooster, is Registered in U.S. Patent and Trademark Office and in other countries. Marca Registrada. Bantam Books, 1540 Broadway, New York, New York 10036.

PRINTED IN THE UNITED STATES OF AMERICA

RAD   0 9 8 7 6 5 4 3

WAGONTONGUE

Chapter One

Isaac Jefford had never seen a town he really liked. A man of ingrained faith, he always saw the hand of God plainest when he climbed across the West Texas hills and rode through the tall bluestem of the grassy valleys, when he forded the broad rivers or splashed a horse across the crooked creeks with their laughing water cool and clear.

To him a town was a place of too many strangers, a thing of noise and clutter and trash, a scar on the face of the land like a pimple on the bosom of a beautiful woman. Dry Wells was no exception.

He stood inside the corral, watching a dozen young horses stir restlessly, their hoofs raising dry dust that floated lazily, for there was not enough wind to carry it away. The horse trader sat atop the raw board fence, his spurred bootheels hooked over a plank. "Isaac, the Major knows his horses. He can be right proud of this bunch he's bought here."

Standing beneath the trader, Isaac nodded without enthusiasm. "I expect he is, if he got them at his price."

"Mighty near his price. We all got to make a livin', but I compromise for a good customer like the Major."

Isaac leaned back against the fence and contemplated a mean-eyed little bay that showed a considerable amount of Mexico blood. He knew a bunch of Major Lytton's cowboys who might not be quite so proud of these new horses. "That bay yonder, I bet he can jump twelve feet straight up from a standin' start."

The trader spat a brown stream of tobacco juice out into the corral. "Might be one or two in there with a little rough edge that still needs a mite of polish, but them is solid ponies, Isaac, as good as you'll find from here to the Pecos River. I wouldn't give two bits for a horse that didn't pitch a little at the beginnin'. Anyway, they ought not to scare *you* any. You're as good a bronc stomper as any man ever I seen, white *or* black."

Isaac broke into a smile, his teeth ivory white against the black of his face. "I reckon everybody has got to have *somethin'* he can do."

"I always wondered why you do it, Isaac. Not many nig— . . . not many fellers of your persuasion take up with the broncs. Looks to me like you'd find it a lot less dangerous pickin' cotton."

Isaac shrugged. "It's a sittin'-down job."

Trader Cunningham chuckled and climbed off the fence, pausing to pick a splinter from the seat of his dusty britches. "If ever you get tired of workin' for the Major out on that old Big Lonesome, you come to see me, Isaac."

Isaac shook his head. "I been with the Major since I was a boy. I doubt as I'll want to leave. But thank you." Through the plank fence he could see the rude sprawl of the town beyond the confines of this straw-strewn wagonyard. It had always made him uneasy. It was a place of strangers, a place where no one knew him for who or what he was, where not more than a dozen men even knew his name or gave a damn. To most of the town he was simply *that darky of the Major's,* of no more interest or importance than the Major's horse or the Major's dog.

There were no strangers at the ranch; there he knew everybody, and everybody knew him. He could breathe easily. He knew where he stood.

The trader said, "You ain't fixin' to take them ponies out of here this evenin', are you, Isaac? You're welcome to sleep in the wagonyard tonight. Be a chance for you to drink some good whiskey and have a little fun."

Isaac couldn't remember that he had ever had much fun in this town or any other. "The outfit needs these broncs. Been too many got crippled since the roundup started. Me and Alvin Quain brought a wagon to get supplies at Mister Handley's store. Soon as Mister Handley gets them all laid out, I'll come for these ponies and we'll start back."

"Seems a shame, Isaac, rememberin' my own cowboy days, and how I'd sweat for months to get a day or two in town."

Isaac was sure the horse trader really meant it. "Orders from the wagonboss. If we make the south linecamp by tonight, we'll get to the roundup by tomorrow evenin'."

"Well, Isaac, I know you'll do what you think is best."

"I always try to, Mister Cunningham."

Cunningham turned his attention back to the ponies. "You figurin' on ridin' one of them new ones and drivin' the rest?"

Isaac shook his head. "I figured I'd ride the same one I come to town on. He ain't worked enough to hurt him."

"A pity. I'd hoped to see you get on that bay. Ain't often we get much excitement around here."

Isaac figured he would get plenty of chance to ride that bay, but he would do it out on the ranch where people wouldn't figure he was trying to show off, and where nobody would laugh—much—if he busted his tail. He had never liked to make a show for people, especially people he didn't know or care about.

It wasn't far down to the general store where he and Quain had pulled the wagon up to the loading dock, but Isaac didn't walk. He went to the dun horse he had tied outside the corral, swung into the saddle, and rode the short distance. He had spent the larger part of his life around cowcamps, and most cowboys wouldn't walk to the toilet if they had a horse tied by the back door.

He saw that the storekeeper had already placed a number of items on the dock . . . some flour in barrels, some sacks of salt, some wooden boxes that contained packages of coffee beans. Isaac pulled the dun up close and stepped directly from the saddle onto the dock, tying the reins to the steel rod which held the wagon's tailgate in place. The grocer came out with a heavy sack in his arms. Isaac said, "If you've got this stuff counted, Mister

Handley, me and Alvin Quain will start puttin' it in the wagon."

The grocer set the sack down, breathing hard, and dusted his apron. "I reckon you'll put it in the wagon by yourself, Isaac. Quain left here when you went down to the wagonyard. Said he'd be gone an hour or so."

Isaac frowned. "Where'd he go?"

The storekeeper glanced down the street. "If you needed him real bad, I'd say you could find him at Big Bessie's. But I don't think you want him. He strikes me as a man with a raw temper."

Worriedly Isaac said, "I promised the wagonboss we wouldn't be gone a bit longer than was needful." He stared at the wheel-rutted street. Down yonder a couple of blocks, hidden by other buildings, was Big Bessie's place, a couple of large rooms in front, then a long hall with a single row of rooms opening into it on one side. Normally Big Bessie wouldn't let Isaac Jefford past the front door, but a couple of times he had had to go down there and fetch some Bar L cowboy who had drunk too much to walk out on his own. He didn't like the place; it smelled of bad whiskey and cheap powder and sweat. It stirred up hungers he could not afford even to admit to, much less to satisfy. "Maybe it won't take him long. I doubt as he's got a dollar with him. None of us been paid since the last time we was in town."

The storekeeper was a tall, rope-thin man whose shoulders had begun to sag as the years piled upon him. Like many another merchant he had no intention of living in this cowtown all his life. Soon as he had made enough money out of the place he would turn his back on it and go to some larger town that offered more in the way of comforts, like Fort Worth or Dallas or Waco. "Then he'll be along directly. Old Bessie never heard of credit." His little gray moustache tugged at the corners in a faint suggestion of a smile. "I don't reckon you've ever been bothered with that affliction."

"What's that, Mister Handley?"

"Bessie's trade. Not much opportunity for *you* out in this country."

"No sir."

"Well, don't worry yourself. When you get to my

age and look back, you'll see there wasn't much to it anyhow. You want to help me with some big sacks of beans?"

Isaac had never warmed to Handley as he had done to the horse trader Cunningham, for he knew of no common interest with the man. But he enjoyed walking into the store. To a man used to spending his time out with a chuckwagon or in a Spartan cowcamp where the food ran strictly to staples like bread, beef, and beans, a place like this made a man's mouth water. Isaac's needs were simple; he seldom spent money for anything except an occasional change of clothes, a pair of boots, and a little smoking tobacco. When he came to town this way, which was seldom, he liked to debauch himself on a sack of rock candy and maybe a can or two of peaches. He could take whiskey or leave it alone; he had never been exposed to enough of it to get him in any trouble.

The beans weren't all that heavy for Isaac, though he supposed they would strain a man of Handley's long years and spare frame. Waving the storekeeper away, he hoisted the sack over his strong shoulder and carried it out onto the dock, dropping it directly into the bed of the wagon. When Isaac went back in, he found Handley frowning over a half-wadded sheet of paper.

Handley said, "You-all got a new cook out at your chuckwagon?"

"No sir, it's still old Wash."

"Well, he's either gettin' bolder in his old age or the Major is gettin' softer. There's not a wagon cook in this whole territory has got the nerve to order out a case of canned peaches."

Isaac had picked up another sack of beans, but he set it down. "Peaches? There wasn't no peaches on that list."

"They're there, as plain as the wart on an old maid's chin."

"But I wrote out that list for Wash; you know he can't read or write. He didn't ask for no peaches, and I sure didn't write none down."

The storekeeper handed Isaac the sheet, and Isaac laboriously ran his finger down the list, his lips moving as he slowly read off the items to himself. There it was, at

the bottom, *1 case peches.* Isaac knew it wasn't his handwriting. Whoever had written it had misspelled the word;
he was certain it should have a double *e.* "I didn't write
this on here, and Wash couldn't."

"Then it was added later. Who else had his hands on
the list?"

Isaac started to say that nobody had, but he remembered that Alvin Quain had brought the list to town in
his shirt pocket because he was driving the wagon.

Handley said, "We'd best leave the peaches off,
then."

"No sir, there's a chance Joe Sample, the wagonboss, put it on there. Major might've told him he figured
on bringin' cattle buyers to the wagon and they needed
this stuff for a special big cobbler pie or somethin'. Best
not take no chance of disagreeables with the Major."
Isaac frowned over the list. It called for three barrels of
flour. He would almost swear that when he wrote it the
list had said two. Maybe he was wrong; the way old
Wash gossiped and rambled on while he was working out
the list, a man could forget.

Handley said, "When you get back to camp, you tell
the Major about the peaches."

"The Major won't be back for a few days. He come
here and bought some horses, then went off on a trip to
see about a cattle buyer."

"If there's any question, though, you tell him how it
was. I don't want him raisin' hell with me. I need his
trade."

"And I need the job."

Handley sniffed. "Major Lytton ain't goin' to fire
you, Isaac. He keeps you around like a pet dog."

Isaac tried to keep the sudden anger from rising in
his face. He wanted to say *I do a man's work; there's no
charity in it,* but he held back. No good end would be
served in showing anger to Handley; the merchant would
resent a black man speaking up to him. He would probably pass word to the Major, and Isaac would get one of
the Major's short, fatherly lectures about observing the
proprieties. Isaac knew how to stay out of trouble.

He picked up the sack of beans again and carried it
to the wagon, looking vainly for a sign of Quain's return.

He loaded the wagon by himself. When the job was finished, Quain still had not shown up. Isaac felt a prickling of impatience to be on his way, but he knew he wouldn't go hunting for Quain. That would be overstepping his bounds.

"I was thinkin', Mister Handley, if you don't need that list I ought to take it back with me. Joe Sample might want to check it over."

The storekeeper handed him the sheet of paper. Isaac crammed it into his shirt pocket along with a sack of smoking tobacco he had bought with his own money. Handley said, "I don't need it noway. I got my own invoice here for Quain to sign when he gets back."

"I can sign it for you."

The old man studied Isaac dubiously. "I'll wait for Quain."

Isaac managed not to anger this time. He had been with the Major much of his life; Quain had been working for the Bar L only six months. Isaac was an all-around cowboy; he could do just about any job which needed doing. Quain was no cowboy; he mostly drove the "hoodlum" wagon and did odd jobs that took no particular skill. But Isaac supposed it was to be expected that Handley would look to Quain to sign the invoice; that was the way things were in this world. It wasn't that Handley meant Isaac any harm; he just didn't mean him any particular good. That was one reason Isaac didn't care much about coming to town.

Isaac said, "Maybe it'd be better if Alvin Quain *did* sign it."

Directly Quain showed up, walking a little unsteadily. It was plain to see he had been drinking some down at Bessie's. A broad-shouldered man with a little of a paunch, he made a half-hearted attempt to climb up onto the dock from the ground, then gave it up and walked around to the end. He grunted in complaint as he labored up the wooden steps. His round, vein-reddened face showed streaks of sweat from the walk and the exertion, and the whiskey.

Isaac thought idly, *If Big Bessie don't give credit, I wonder where he got the money?*

Quain looked a moment at the wagon. He could see

it was ready, but he said in a curt and commanding voice, "Get her loaded up, Isaac."

Isaac didn't even frown. "It's all ready to go, Mister Quain."

Quain's voice was sharp. "You damn sure you didn't leave nothin' out?"

You know damn well I didn't, Isaac thought, but he said, "Mister Handley checked ever bit of it. He wants you to sign the invoice before we leave." Isaac watched as Quain did so, and he noted that the man wrote slowly, agonizing over every letter. He thought, *That's something else I can do better than you,* but he never considered saying it out loud.

Quain said, "I've decided them mules need a rest. I'm goin' to spend the night in town and start out in the mornin'."

Gently Isaac reminded him, "Joe Sample said we was to start back as soon as we got the business done."

Quain's eyes were suddenly angry and challenging. "Boy, you tryin' to tell me what to do?"

Isaac moved back a step. "No sir, I'm just sayin' what Joe Sample told us. It ain't me tellin' you nothin', it's *him*."

"What he don't know ain't goin' to hurt him none."

"He'll know when we don't show up by tomorrow evenin'."

Quain clenched his fist. "You watch yourself, Isaac, or I'll take down a piece of that rope yonder and flay me about ten pounds of black hide."

The storekeeper took a step forward. "Quain, I don't want no trouble here. You-all want to fight, you go do it somewhere else. Isaac, you hear me?"

Isaac moved back a couple more steps. "I ain't after no trouble. I was just tellin' him what Joe Sample said."

Quain pointed a stubby finger at Isaac. "You go see after your horses, boy. You leave a white man to white man's business."

Isaac saw nothing else he could do; he couldn't afford to fight Quain, especially not here in town among strangers. He untied his horse and stepped directly off the dock into his scarred old saddle. He turned the dun back down toward the wagonyard. He could hear Quain still cursing behind him.

The horse trader opened the gate and held it, letting Isaac ride into the pen without dismounting. Cunningham said, "Looked to me like you was havin' some trouble over yonder."

"I *could* of had. I backed away."

"That's best in the long run, Isaac."

"Man like me gets used to backin' away," Isaac said bitterly.

"It's a hard world for all of us, one way or another. If it was me, I could stomp on him. But you can't afford to. Just hold off long enough and you'll have the satisfaction of seein' somebody else stomp him. Save yours for the broncs, Isaac. You'll stay a whole lot healthier."

"I reckon," Isaac replied.

He was uneasy under the trader's thoughtful gaze. Seemed like he never could tell what a white man was thinking. Cunningham jerked his head. "Come on into the barn."

Isaac followed him through the big door, which had been built wide enough to accept a freight wagon. There was no office, but in a corner away from the stalls and the hay was a rolltop desk and three or four rawhide chairs, two of them lying on the ground. The trader said, "I got a bottle in here someplace." He rummaged around in a drawer and came up with it. He held it up to the light, frowning. "Damn near empty. That old swamper has found my hidin' place." He uncorked it and took a long swallow, then handed the bottle to Isaac. "Finish that. I hate to see a hard-workin' man leave town dry."

Isaac tipped the bottle up until it was empty. "Thank you, Mister Cunningham. That was mighty good."

The trader shrugged. "Everybody ain't like Alvin Quain."

Isaac moved around the ponies, hazing them toward the gate. The trader waved his arm to keep the wild-eyed bay from circling back around the lot. In the dusty wake of the ponies, Cunningham swung the gate shut and stood there, watching them string out up the street. "Come back, Isaac. You're welcome *here* anytime."

Pushing the ponies past the Handley store, Isaac made it a point not to glance in Quain's direction. But once past, he looked back over his shoulder and saw Quain pull the wagon away from the dock. The man didn't put the team in the direction the broncs and Isaac had taken. He pulled them around and headed the other way.

Back to Bessie's, Isaac thought. *Now I know how he figures to pay what he owes her.*

Chapter Two

Major Estel Lytton sat alone at an unused poker table and tried not to look at the dark-whiskered man who glowered at him from a shadowy corner of the lamp-lighted saloon. For half an hour the Major had been aware of the hostile scrutiny, and he had tried to figure out where or if he had ever seen the man before. He had made enemies through the years—more than enough to go around—but he had known about them at the time. If he had ever met this man, he could not remember it. Possibly the war . . . possibly the years had changed the man, and the whiskers masked the face.

Major Lytton emptied his glass and glanced up to see the bartender watching for a sign he wanted another drink. The Major nodded and the barman came out from behind the old walnut bar with an open bottle in his hand. As he poured the glass full, the Major said, "Don't make a show of it, but take a look at the man in the corner. Do you know him?"

The bartender didn't have to look. "No, I can't say as ever I seen him before. I figured you knew him, the way he's been burnin' a hole in you."

"He's a stranger to me. What do you take him for?"

"I figured him for a cowpuncher when he walked in here. Kind of hard-used lately, from the looks of him. You sure you don't know him? He acts like he sure as hell knows *you.*"

The Major shook his head and motioned that the glass was full enough. Of a sudden he was losing his taste for whiskey.

"Do you have any law in this town?"

"This ain't a county seat. We got a deputy sheriff, but he's out tryin' to track down some horses."

"No other law?"

"Not unless you'd count a little cavalry detail that rode in before dark. Lieutenant took him a room over at the *ho*-tel. Six or seven of them black buffalo soldiers, they're puttin' up at the wagonyard. You think you'd be needin' them?"

"I never called on a federal soldier to do anything except surrender. Lord, if I could just remember this man, then maybe I'd know what his trouble is."

The bartender leaned closer. "Occurs to me maybe he don't know you atall. Occurs to me maybe he thinks you look like a man with money on you, and he's got it in his mind to rob you."

That uneasy thought had occurred to the Major, too. He had been robbed once. For years he had ridden thousands of miles over unknown ranges carrying saddlebags full of money without being bothered, but once he was robbed of his wallet and seventeen dollars by a footpad in a dark street of a jerkwater town about like this one, within a block of a jailhouse, a sheriff, and two deputies.

Now the possibility stared him in the face again. He scowled, angry for allowing himself to be cornered into a situation like this. He could as easily have taken his evening whiskey in the bar of the hotel, but he had wanted to get out and stretch his legs in the night air. Now here he was in a second-rate saloon at the far end of a dark street, two blocks from his hotel, without even a pistol for self-protection.

He guessed he looked like a man who would be carrying money, all right. He had been down south to talk to cattle buyer Lon Whitten about this fall's steers. He had always considered it wise in such a situation to look prosperous. If a man appeared to need money, a cattle buyer—even a friend like Lon—was more likely to take advantage of him.

Major Lytton was a man in his late fifties, his hair and heavy moustache mostly gray, his cheeks jowlier than they used to be, his belt three notches wider than when he rode at the head of a troop of cavalry battling across Virginia. Those had been bold and bloody days when he stood in fear of no man.

He felt no fear of the man who watched him from the corner, but rather annoyance and an angry helplessness. He had no sword now, no black charger, no braid. He was becoming certain that when he got up from this whiskey-stained table and ventured out into the darkness this man would come upon him with a gun in his hand and hold him as powerless as a worm on a hook. It wasn't just the money; he didn't really have all that much on him. More, it was the ignominy of being subjugated by a man of no account, a common skulking thief.

He sat sipping the whiskey, considering how he might outwit the man. He could not leave here without being seen. All this man had to do was outwait him. He could ask the bartender for protection, but that idea repelled him; the barman was a stranger and owed him nothing, certainly not a personal risk. Finally, he could send for the army's help, but that too went against all his inclinations. Though the war was long since over, he could never quite shake a deeply ingrained feeling that this was the enemy, these men in the blue uniforms with the yellow stripe down the legs. He could imagine a situation in which they might look good to him, but it would have to be an emergency much larger than a common footpad out to lift a wallet.

He asked the bartender, "Could you lend me a pistol?"

The bartender said regretfully, "There's not a weapon in the place. Boss says a gun in a saloon just brings trouble on the barkeep."

A plan began to shape itself. Seated at a table halfway across the room were two men, possibly drummers. By their look the Major did not take them to be cowboys, but he had seen a pistol in the waistband of one when he reached across the table for a bottle. The other probably was armed also, though the Major had not seen a weapon. He had seen them glance his way a time or two, and their manner had seemed friendly enough.

Very well, he would sit here and wait until they were ready to go. When they left, he would go out on their heels and stick close to them. If they went to the hotel, fine. If it turned out they were not going his way, he would quickly and quietly lay his cards on the table. Surely they would not refuse him in this situation, and he thought it unlikely that a robber would dare take on three men in the darkness. If ever he made the hotel, he would have the use of the pistol he kept in his saddle-bags. Then a common thief would play hell getting the edge on Major Estel Lytton!

So he sat, keeping an eye on the two men for a sign they were about to get up and go. Now and again he glanced surreptitiously at the man in the corner, and always it seemed the man's unfriendly eyes met his. The Major smouldered in resentment that he should be kept here this way, virtually a prisoner at the pleasure of such a man.

He quit sipping the whiskey, simply lifting the glass to his lips once in a while to make a show of it; he had no intention of letting his reflexes be blunted even a little. Impatience gnawed as he glanced frequently at the two men he was depending upon to get him out of this. Damn them, didn't a couple of drummers have anything better to do than sit here and drink all night and smoke up the place with strong tobacco? Once in a while he reached in his vest pocket for the silver watch he carried, checking the time. It was crowding midnight. Weren't they ever going to get up?

Even more than the money, he hated the thought of losing the watch. It wasn't so much the sentiment of the thing, it was the cost; he had paid two hundred dollars for it in Kansas City. A man didn't come upon a watch like this just anywhere these days. He disconnected the chain carefully, and when he sensed that the man in the corner had looked away to some distraction, he quickly slipped the watch into his boottop, just in case.

Finally the two men at the table stood up. They moved slowly to the door and stepped out into the night. Major Lytton pushed his chair aside and came to his feet, letting the chair fall back and hit the rough floor with a clatter. The sound startled him, but he tried not to show it. He strode directly for the door. From the corner of his eye, he saw the man in the corner getting up.

Well, by God, it's now or never. He moved away from the front-porch lantern light and saw the two men walking like vague shadows. Relief came over him with a rush; they were moving toward the hotel. He stepped quickly, hoping to catch up to them without making any commotion about it. He did not look back, but a sixth sense set the hair to bristling at the back of his neck. He knew the lone man was outside now, probably following him. He moved a little faster, though he took pains not to strike a trot.

The watch had slipped down to the ankle inside his right boot, and it rubbed hard and painfully. It was all he could do to avoid limping, perhaps giving the thing away.

Moving into a patch of almost total darkness by the tall frame wall of the livery barn, he glanced back and saw nothing.

A voice spoke in front of him. "If you'll take that watch out of your boot, you can walk a little easier."

He found himself face to face with a man who was little more than shadow . . . two men, in fact. But it wasn't the men he noticed so much as the big round bore of a snub-nosed pistol one of them held. The man spoke again, "I say there, friend, it'll ease your pain considerable if you'll shed yourself of that good watch. I'll do you a favor and take it. And I seen that wallet you flashed in yonder. We'll take that too, and lighten your burden."

Major Lytton was dry-mouthed, taken totally by surprise. Even in the darkness he could see that these were the men he had counted on to help him, the two he had followed out of the saloon.

Goddamn! he thought. *A man can't depend on anything anymore!*

The second holdup man said, "We know you ain't got no gun, but you reach down and get that watch real easy just the same. We'd hate to have to kill a man over somethin' so trivial."

The Major fetched up the watch and placed it in an outstretched hand. Anger welled in his throat, and he began to curse, partly against them, partly against himself. He had walked into this like a blind badger into a trap.

"No need cussin' *us*," one of the men said. "There ain't nothin' personal on our part. We just got to make a livin', is all."

"You could *work* for it," the Major replied brittlely, "like everybody else does."

"Hard work makes a man old before his time."

A third voice spoke from the darkness. "You'll die young if you don't change your ways, boys."

The man with the pistol whirled around, but not in time. Lytton caught a blur of movement and heard a hard crunch. A hat went flying, and the man fell flat on his stomach. The pistol bounced across the bare ground. Stooping quickly, the Major grabbed it up.

Now he saw the bewhiskered man who had glared at him all night. He held a big six-shooter he had used as a club.

The second thief wasted no motions. He turned suddenly and sprinted off into the darkness, fast as a jackrabbit. The Major's benefactor fired at him twice but without evident effect. "Missed him," the man muttered. "Just too damned dark. Maybe it's just as well. I don't care to go to jail for shootin' a two-bit thief. This here one is the bird that got your stuff, ain't he?"

"He's the one," the Major said, kneeling, retrieving his wallet and his watch from the man's pockets. "Could be you broke his head. He's out colder than a wedge."

"It'll leave an impression on him. He'll study on it some the next time he goes out to rob a man in the dark of the night."

In the darkness came the sounds of running feet. Several Negro soldiers climbed over the wagonyard fence and jumped to the ground, most of them only half dressed. They had been sleeping in the shed. "What's goin' on out here?" demanded one with two stripes on the sleeve of his wide-open shirt.

The man with the whiskers told him, "Nothin' for you burr-headed soldier boys to get yourselves in a bother about. Go on back to bed."

The corporal knelt beside the fallen man. "Has he been shot?"

The Major said, "No, but he's probably got a knot on his head the size of a duck egg. He set out to rob me."

"What was the shootin' about?"

"There was another one. He got away in the dark."

The corporal said, "The lieutenant will want to hear about this. You men stay here."

The man who had rescued Lytton said crisply, "Who you orderin' around, boy?"

"I was talkin' to you, sir." The corporal's tone became a little less commanding.

"You see any uniform on me?"

"No sir."

"That means you got no authority to tell me what to do. I don't take orders off of no military son-of-a-bitch, and most especially off of no *black* military son-of-a-bitch. You hear me, soldier?"

The corporal let out a long slow breath, studying the man warily. "If you don't mind, sir. I think the lieutenant would probably like to talk to you. At your convenience, of course."

The Major decided his benefactor was on the verge of saying too much, if he hadn't already. "Corporal, tell your lieutenant that if he wants us he can find us in the hotel bar. I owe this man a drink. As for the other man," he motioned toward the one trying to crawl on the ground, "do with him what you will. I have lost all interest in him."

"Yes sir," said the corporal. He posted two of the men to watch the would-be robber while the rest repaired to the barn to finish getting their clothes on. The corporal trotted toward the hotel, shoving his shirttail into his britches.

The stranger said, "You don't owe me nothin'. I'd of done the same if it had been one of them black troopers instead of you. Just never could stand a thief."

"Nor can I stand to remain in someone's debt. I'd be pleased to buy you a drink. A whole bottle, or even a keg."

"We sat in that saloon together half the night and you never offered me no drink."

"Not together, exactly. Anyway, I didn't know you then."

"You don't know me now."

"You're right. I am Major Estel Lytton." He extended his hand.

The other man pondered awhile before he took it, and even then he didn't grip with any enthusiasm. "I'm Pete Runyan."

Lytton frowned. "I get an uncomfortable feeling you don't like me."

"Can't say as I do."

"But you don't know me. Or *do* you?"

"Never laid eyes on you till tonight."

"Then why did you come to help me out?"

"There's three things in this world I got no use for. One is a thief, another is a rich damyankee, and the third is a triflin' darky. In about that order."

"You have taken me for a rich Yankee?"

"It's the way you've got, the way you walk and the clothes you wear and the whole air about you, like you was somebody come and the rest of us didn't amount to much."

Lytton shook his head. "I'm afraid you've jumped to a fast and faulty conclusion. There is a rich and greedy Fort Worth banker named J. Warren Norris who knows that I am a long way from being a rich man. In fact, if I hadn't just finished an arrangement to sell my steers in time to make a payment to him, I would be an exceedingly poor man overnight."

"A poor man is as a poor man does, and you don't do like no poor man."

"I'd still be pleased to buy you that drink."

"If it'll ease your conscience any. . . ." Pete Runyan started walking, and the Major stepped up to stay beside him. He wondered what Runyan thought he needed his conscience eased for, but he didn't ask. As they walked up onto the plank porch of the frame hotel Runyan said, "It ain't so fancy a place when you get up close and take a real look at it."

"Are you staying at the hotel, Runyan?"

Runyan grimaced. "Hell, I ain't even stayin' at the wagonyard. I got my horse staked out yonder aways. "I'm sleepin' on the prairie."

The Major stared at him in surprise. "I'd be glad to pay for a room for you."

"Why?"

"To get you in out of the night."

"When a man ain't used to somethin' it don't bother him not to have it. Sleepin' in a *ho*-tel would just give me big notions, and I couldn't live up to them. The night air is free, and I ain't beholden to nobody."

The Major knew a stubborn man when he saw one, and he sure as hell saw one. He walked into the hotel's small bar, where the trade was slow and the tables plentiful. He picked one where he could see the lobby and be seen. He figured that the lieutenant would be looking for him. "This suit you?" he asked Runyan.

"You're payin' for it. Pick to suit yourself."

He ordered whiskey and glasses, and the chunky, red-faced barman brought them. The Major lifted his glass in salute. "My thanks."

Runyan grunted. He critically tasted the whiskey, trying a little of it as if he thought they might try to poison him. "Ain't bad," he conceded reluctantly and emptied his glass in one swallow that twisted his face like a wrung-out lemon.

The Major asked, "You need a job?"

"I ain't beggin' for nothin'."

The man was somewhat younger than the Major had originally thought, looking at him in the dark shadows of that saloon. He placed him within a couple of years of thirty, one side or the other; this country aged men in different ways, so it was hard to tell for sure. Runyan frowned at the whiskey glass, his gray eyes half belligerent. He hadn't shaved in a couple of weeks, but the relative evenness of his whiskers indicated that when he felt like it he shaved clean except for a moustache.

Lytton tried again. "I'd take you for a cowboy."

"You got some feelin' against cowboys?"

"None atall. I get along fine with cowboys. In fact, I could use another one or two. I have a ranch above here, and we've got the chuckwagon out, and I'm short-handed."

Runyan scowled. "You're probably one of them damyankees that play-acts at ranchin'—that works a man till his butt drags the ground, and feeds him poorly and pays him worse."

Lytton began to nettle. "Do not call me a Yankee, sir. I commanded cavalry in Hood's Brigade in the late war, and if there had been a few more of us we'd have driven those Yankees into the ocean. Call me what you will, but do not call me a Yankee."

"Damned officer, just the same. Me, I was a private and proud to say it."

Lytton's mouth went hard. "Well, if you don't want a job . . ."

"I didn't say that. Hell yes, I want a job. But I want it understood that I ain't beggin' for one, and I ain't kissin' nobody's soft bottom to get one. When I work for a man, all I'm givin' him is my time. He don't in noways own me. He don't tell me nothin' except what pertains to my work, and that work is goin' to be good."

The Major stared at him in angry impatience. "Now, I've met some ingrates in my time. . . ."

"Ingrates? Hell, who was it done *who* a favor? I saved you from losin' your britches; all you've done for me is to buy me a drink."

Not often had the Major gone out of his way to offer someone a job; usually men came to *him*, and they never made conditions. He had always accepted the premise that the man who paid the wages made the conditions. He was on the verge of telling Pete Runyan to go to hell.

But there was a sardonic streak in Major Lytton, and he paused. The anger faded; he found himself intrigued by the brass of this man. He had often noted during the war that the contrary and the contentious usually came through when the pinch was on. He had always been fond of saying that he admired a man of independent spirit, though he could not recall that he had ever appreciated this spirit when it was applied against him. He found himself wondering whether this was deepseated, or if the fire was simply fueled by the night's whiskey. The chill of early morning might find the fire out and the ashes dead. He said, "You never did tell me if you're a cowboy or not."

"Don't I look like one?"

"Anybody can look like one if he puts his mind to it. To tell you the truth, while we were sitting in that other saloon I took you for a holdup man. I thought those other two were drummers."

That was like tossing a bucketful of kerosene on an open flame. The longer Runyan thought about it, the angrier he became. "You took *me* for one of *them*?" His fists clenched, and for a moment Lytton thought he would have to protect himself. Runyan shoved his chair back and poised there like a cat pondering whether to spring. "If I'd of known that, I'd of let them rob you."

Lytton shrugged. "It was the way you kept looking at me . . . the same way you're looking at me now."

Runyan eased. "I reckon I had cause . . . you sittin' there like a rich somebody up on the hill, and me so broke that every time I walk by a dog it lifts its hind leg at me."

Lytton poured Runyan's glass full. "I was wrong about you and you were wrong about me. The job offer still stands; I owe you that."

"You owe me nothin'. If I was to work for you it'd be because I'm good at my job, and not because you owe it to me."

"Fair enough."

"I always pull my end of the load and a little bit more. I ain't one to brag, but I'm as good a hand as *you'll* ever see. You'll pay me good wages and I'll earn them. There won't nobody be givin' nothin' away . . . not you and not me."

"It's a deal, Pete Runyan. You might even get to like me."

"Damned small chance of that."

Chapter Three

The broncs plodded in a ragged double file a respectable distance behind Alvin Quain's hoodlum wagon, and Isaac Jefford poked along behind the broncs, forcing down his natural impatience to pick up and be moving. Quain would not hear to having the broncs pass on ahead; he said he did not intend to eat their dust. Isaac figured at the rate the wagon was moving he would soon be so far ahead of it that the dust would be settled by the time the wagon got there. But it was in his training not to argue much, or question what he was told. Whatever resentment he harbored—and it was considerable—he held within himself.

He had reached the line shack with the broncs before dark last night. Quain had not arrived with the wagon until much later; he had spent a long time in town. He ordered Isaac out of the shack and commandeered it for his own use. Isaac slept outdoors. That was no particular hardship—he did it several months of the year—but it was galling to give way to a narrow-gauge man like Alvin Quain. If it had been the Major or Joe Sample, he would have deferred on his own without giving the matter any consideration.

They stopped at noon to fix a little chuck. Isaac did the work while Quain sat pulling at a bottle of cheap whiskey. Isaac figured Quain was trying to finish it so there would be time for the smell to wear off before he reached the main camp. He offered none of the whiskey, which suited Isaac just as well. He figured it was diluted by Quain's tobacco juice. Quain stared while Isaac set a pot of coffee on his small fire and went about slicing bacon from a slab to eat with the cold biscuits he had baked at the line cabin last night.

Quain said, "I don't understand what you're doin' out here in the first place, Isaac, in a cow outfit like this'n. Why ain't you back east pickin' cotton?"

Isaac shrugged. "The Major ain't got no cotton. He's just got cows."

"There's other people to work for besides the Major."

"Not for me. I been with him ever since I was a little bit of a kid."

"He owned you once, didn't he?"

"Back when there was still slaves, he owned me."

"When the war was over and you was free, why didn't you light out for yourself? There was no law to make you stay with him."

"Law said I was free to do what I wanted to. I wanted to stay with the Major."

Quain snorted. "Afraid, that's what I think. I think you was afraid to go out and face the world by yourself; you hung onto him like a big old boy afraid to go off and leave his mamma."

Isaac's hand went tight on the bail of the coffeepot, and he turned so Quain couldn't see the irritation rushing into his face. "The Major's always been good to me."

"Why not? He owns you like he owns his cows."

"I ain't no slave. He pays me wages like everybody else."

"Does he? Does he pay you as much as he pays everybody else?"

Isaac didn't answer that. Quain answered it for himself. "Naturally he don't. Take a bunch of cowhides to the tanner and he'll pay less for the black hides than for the white ones."

"I ain't no slave."

"Ain't you?"

When the coffee was ready Quain poured a cup and sat back to drink it while he waited for Isaac to get the bacon fried. He sipped it and made a heavy face. "You call this coffee?" He poured what was left of the whiskey into his cup. "You're a damn poor cook."

"I never made no claim. Cookin' is Wash's job."

Quain scowled. "He's even blacker'n *you* are. I swear, I don't see why they don't run both of you back to the cottonfields. You got no business workin' out here amongst *men*."

Isaac turned away and let his imagination run wild. He pictured himself breaking a shovel over Quain's head and telling everybody the man had died drunk, falling out of the wagon. This was a way Isaac had of letting off steam when the pressure got strong: dream up ways he could take revenge without getting caught. He never considered carrying the schemes through. They were simply a relief valve, a way of assuring himself that he had the power if he ever really wanted to use it, a way of gaining equality in his own mind without doing anything overt that might make him vulnerable. He had killed many a man who needed it . . . in his mind. He had dug their graves deep and filled them up and pounded the dirt in their faces. And as they went on their way unaware, Isaac could look at them with a secret sense of mastery and say to himself, *You're only walkin' around because I decided to let you.* Tolerance came easier then.

Isaac would admit that Quain was right on one point: he was not much of a cook. He was hungry long before they reached camp a while short of sundown. He could see that the hands were at the chuckwagon waiting for Wash to finish supper, except three men left with the herd, and the horse wrangler. They began drifting out afoot to meet him, and a couple of men trotted to open a gate into a set of rough corrals built of brush. Isaac circled the broncs well around Wash's chuckwagon to avoid stirring dust into the supper, and he put them into the corral in a brisk trot. A cowboy rushed into their dusty wake and closed the gate behind them.

Isaac glanced at the wagon and saw the bent-shouldered black cook standing behind the chuckbox lid, looking at him. *Get to work, Wash,* he thought; *I could eat the hind quarters off of a stray bull.* But nobody hurried Wash if he didn't want to be hurried, and he seldom did.

Joe Sample walked through the drifting veil of dust and raised his hand in a greeting of sorts. " 'Bout gave you up, Isaac."

Isaac could have told the wagonboss the straight of it, but he chose not to. "Wagon's pretty well loaded, Mister Joe, and we couldn't rush it."

Sample walked on to the fence and looked between the upright mesquite branches and trunks which had been sunk a few inches into the ground and bound together with rawhide. He was a tall, skinny man not much short of fifty. "What do you think of the horses, Isaac?"

"I don't never fault the Major. Whatever he picks to buy, that sets mighty fine with me."

Sample stared at the broncs a minute or two, giving each a quick appraisal. Isaac knew Sample's eyes didn't miss much; if there was a blemish or a mark, Sample would know it. His quick eyes and his shrewd judgment had made him the Major's righthand man for years. Isaac considered himself the Major's lefthand man, if there was such a thing. Isaac was the only one here who had been with the Major longer than Joe Sample. "They may not be so fine with you, Isaac, if one of them throws you headfirst into that fence."

Isaac smiled. "Wouldn't be the first time one ever did."

"That bay with his ears up and his eyes wild . . . I'll bet he does."

Isaac marveled sometimes, the way Joe Sample saw things. In a minute or two he had picked the one Isaac had studied all yesterday afternoon and all day today as being probably the roughest in the lot. "I'll bet you fifty cents."

Sample grinned. "Fifty cents." That was the most they ever bet. They had done it for years, and neither man had ever paid the other. They just kept mental note; luck seemed to keep canceling the debts every time they got over a dollar or a dollar and a half. Right now Isaac was standing a dollar ahead.

Most of the cowboys clustered around the fence, looking with a mixture of expectation and apprehension on these horses they would have to try to ride and get a day's work from. Strawboss Hunter Proffitt ran a big strong hand through his rusty hair and pulled his sweat-marked hat down firmly. "Reckon there's any here that'll pitch, Isaac?"

Isaac said, "Reckon there's any that *won't?*"

Proffitt glanced at Joe Sample. "You got a bet on with Isaac about any of them horses?"

"I bet him he can't ride that bay."

Proffitt said, "I'll put up a side bet. I'm with Isaac." He gripped Isaac's shoulder and shook him.

Isaac said nothing; he simply grinned. After spending all that time with Alvin Quain, it was good to be back among friends.

Presently old Wash beat a big tin spoon against the bottom of a pan. The cowboys turned away from the corral and walked back to the wagon, lining up and filing by the chuckbox to pick up their utensils, then working one by one along the line of Dutch ovens and pots.

Isaac held back, waiting until everyone else in camp had his plate, then he went for his own. Some of the men sat on their bedrolls; most squatted in a semicircle on one side of the wagon where they could talk, speculating on the nature of the ponies Isaac had brought to camp. When Isaac had a plateful of food, he went to his accustomed place. He sat on the wagontongue alone. It was a ritual so old he didn't remember where or how or when it had started; it was a way of being with them, yet somehow a little apart. He rode with them all day, worked with them, sweated with them, but he did not eat with them. It was a fine point of distinction he had never questioned or reasoned out. He couldn't remember that anyone had ever required it of him; chances were he had started it himself, so long ago he had forgotten it. Now it was habit, something he was barely conscious of doing.

He sat listening to the talk and smiling to himself as some of the younger hands boasted how they would ride those broncs and never break a sweat. He figured a couple would be lucky if they didn't break an arm.

Old Wash took no food for himself until he saw that everybody else was eating. This was not a matter of being black; it was a matter of being a wagon cook. A cook was always last to eat. Isaac watched him bending over the bean pot, his floursack apron hanging in his way. Wash was short and paunchy, and his kinky hair was mostly gray, a large black island shining on the back of his head. Isaac had no clear idea how old Wash was; fifty or more, old enough that he had grown well into manhood under slavery. He would carry the whip scars to his grave. Wash had never told Isaac how he came to get those marks on his back, and Isaac had never asked him. But he figured those scars explained a lot about Wash.

Wash came over and sat down by Isaac on the wagontongue. It was a thing he seldom did unless he wanted something; Wash was a man who stayed to himself as much as he could. He punched his elbow into Isaac's ribs and whispered, "Did you bring it?"

"Bring what?"

"You know." Wash looked around carefully for a sign anybody might be listening. He whispered, "The whiskey; did you bring it?"

Isaac shook his head. "I told you I wasn't goin' to bring you no whiskey, Wash."

"But I figured your heart would weaken when you got to thinkin' about this poor ol' soul out here alone, thirstin' after somethin' to quench the fires."

"Wash, if I was to've brought you any whiskey, you'd be laid up dead drunk for two days and couldn't cook a lick."

It was hard to tell which hit Wash the hardest, hurt or disappointment. Sad-faced he argued, "What difference would that make? They expect it of black folks, like me and you. Man had just as well live up to what's expected of him."

Isaac chewed his chunk of beef with a vengeance, as if the steer had kicked him. "They may expect it of you, Wash, but they don't expect it of me, and I ain't givin' them any cause to."

Wash's eyes narrowed in anger. "What makes you think they look on you any better than they look on me? Your skin's the same as mine."

Isaac set down his plate. "Maybe so, but there's a lot of ways we're different."

"You think so?" The old man used his words vindictively, poking with them the way he would poke with a sharp stick. "We don't get treated no different, do we? Maybe you see a difference in us, but *they* sure as hell don't. You're black like me, and there ain't no amount of water ever goin' to wash it off." He got up and took his plate out away from the wagon to finish his supper alone.

Isaac looked after him regretfully, wishing he hadn't spoken so bluntly to the old man, but at times it seemed the only way to get through to him was to tell him the straight of it and let the devil take the hindmost. There was a gulf between them he had never quite bridged. The years, for one thing. For another, there was the difference in outlook between a man who had known freedom since early youth and one who had spent part of his manhood in bondage, under the dread of the whip.

Isaac found he wasn't hungry anymore. He walked away from the wagon and emptied his plate in the short grass, wasting the Major's money. He glanced after Wash one more time and thought, *The hell with it.* He dropped his plate into the "wreck" pan, keeping his cup for one more round of coffee. Joe Sample was at the pot when he got there. Hunter Proffitt came up, and Isaac stood back, letting Hunter go ahead of him. "Mister Joe," Isaac asked, "what about them groceries in that wagon?"

Sample shrugged, blowing his coffee. "They can just as well set where they're at till we need the wagon for somethin' else."

Isaac fished into his shirt pocket. "I got the grocery list here. Thought maybe you'd want to check it over and make sure we got everything we was supposed to."

Sample shook his head. "No need to trouble. Old man Handley is as honest as the day is long."

Isaac extended the paper toward Joe Sample. "Mister Joe, it sure might be a good idea to check it anyway." Isaac cast a quick glance at Alvin Quain and saw the big man stand up. Joe Sample saw him too; he sized up the situation as quickly as he had sized up that pen of broncs.

"I expect you're right. Handley's gettin' old; could be he's gettin' careless too."

Quain committed a breach of cow-camp custom that would have earned him stout rebuke from a white wagon cook; he left his plate lying on the ground instead of carrying it to the tub for washing. "Joe," Quain said, trying to look casual about it, "no need to trouble yourself. I checked them goods myself."

Joe Sample ran his finger down the list, his lips moving as he read the items. At the bottom he came to one which made him look up in surprise. "Peaches? What the hell is this? *Peaches?* The Major will throw a fit! Wash . . . ."

Isaac said evenly, "There wasn't no peaches on that list when I wrote it out for Wash. He didn't ask for none, and I didn't write none down."

Joe Sample looked closer at the paper, studying the handwriting.

Quain blinked, his hands beginning to flex nervously. "That damned ol' storekeeper . . . maybe he's gettin' greedy."

Sample shook his head. "Ol' man Handley might steal a thousand cases of peaches, if it ever come handy, but he wouldn't stoop to steal the price of *one.*"

Quain said, "Don't look at me; all I done was drive the wagon. If you ask me, I'd say you better take another look at that Isaac. Them black boys'll all lie, and they'll all steal."

Joe Sample turned. "How about it, Isaac? Did you alter this list?"

"No sir."

"Did Quain do it?"

"I didn't see him."

"But you know he did. Why did he do it, Isaac?"

Isaac hesitated. "He was down at Big Bessie's."

Quain shouted, "You lyin' black son-of-a-bitch." A coiled rope lay on top of a bedroll. Quain shook out enough of it to double back for a whip. Savagely he lashed Isaac across the shoulders. Isaac cried out at the pain, then grabbed the rope. He got both of his big wrists wrapped in it and yanked, burning Quain's hands. Quain let go. Isaac got against Quain and pushed him hard, sending him stumbling back against the hoodlum wagon.

Quain exclaimed, "Don't you lay them black hands on me!" He reached into his pocket and came out with a big pocketknife. Isaac's mouth went dry as the man opened the blade; it was big enough to skin a cow. Quain stepped away from the wagon, jabbing the knife at Isaac. "Boy, I'm fixin' to cut your gizzard out!"

Isaac stepped backward, scared, his eyes on the

blade, his hands held protectively in front of his body. He felt the back of his foot hit against something—a bedroll. He fell backward, seeing triumph in Quain's face, seeing the blade flash at him. As he landed on his back, Isaac had his hands up in front of him, and he caught Quain's wrist, the one that held the knife. He gave it a hard twist, using all the strength he could throw into his arms. Quain gave way, and the blade slashed through his own sleeve. He yelled in surprise and pain.

Joe Sample had picked up the rope where it fell. He dropped the loop over Quain's head and pulled. Choking, Quain had to give up his struggle against Isaac, his hands clawing at the rough rope which burned his neck. One of the cowboys jumped to Sample's aid, and together they jerked Quain backward, half strangling him. Sample kicked the fallen knife away.

"Get on your feet," he commanded sharply. When Quain seemed slow about it, Sample fetched him a hard kick that must have raised a bruise. "Get on your feet, I say!"

Hunter Proffitt knelt worriedly over Isaac. "He didn't cut you none?"

Isaac felt a burning on his wrist and knew the knife had made a good mark. "I'll be all right; I ain't goin' to bleed to death." With Proffitt's help he got to his feet, his heart still beating rapidly. He saw that his sleeve had a long clean rip. "Looks like I need me a needle and thread."

Proffitt said, "We may have to sew *you* up before we worry about that shirt."

Joe Sample held the loop tight on Alvin Quain's neck, cursing him six ways from Sunday. "If you'd of hurt Isaac bad, I swear by God we'd prop up a wagontongue and hang you. Ought to do it anyway, you pullin' a knife on a man."

Quain managed to get his fingers under the rope and pull it loose enough that he could breathe. The red flush stayed in his face. He choked and wheezed and regained his breath. He was surrounded, a creature at bay, but fear had not driven all the anger out of him. "What kind of an outfit is this that takes *his* part against a white man?"

Joe Sample glowered at him. "I don't see no white man. I don't see no man at all. All I see is a petty thief and a knife artist." He loosened the loop but purposely did it roughly enough that he burned Quain's neck again. He lifted the rope over Quain's head. "You're through here. You're leavin' right now."

Quain's gaze moved over the circle of cowboys in search of a friend; he found none. "Somebody catch me a horse."

Sample shook his head. "You had no horse when you joined this outfit. You'll ride none away from here."

Quain's mouth dropped open. "You don't expect me to walk! How'll I carry my saddle and my bedroll?"

"That's somethin' you'll have to work out for yourself."

"You can't just . . ." Quain broke off, for he saw that they could, and that they were going to. "I got wages comin' to me."

Sample went to his bedroll and dug into the warbag he carried there. He came up with a few bills. "This'll have to do. It's all I got with me."

Quain snatched the money from Sample's hand. "I got more comin' to me than that."

"You took the rest of it out in peaches, and whatever else you stole. Now git! If you're still in sight in five minutes, I'll come after you with a bullwhip."

Quain's bed was spread out flat on the ground. He quickly rolled and tied it. It made a considerable bundle, too much for him to carry any great distance, especially with his saddle. He hoisted it onto his shoulder. He turned, his eyes searching out Isaac Jefford. "Boy," he said, voice hard with hatred, "this ain't the end of it. You can't always have this bunch of niggerlovers around you to run to. Sometime—tomorrow, a month from now, next year—I'm goin' to catch you where it's just me and you, and I'm goin' to skin you. I'm goin' to peel that black hide and I'm goin' to make me a tobacco pouch out of it. I'm goin' to let you live long enough to watch me roll the first smoke, and then I'm goin' to kill you!"

Joe Sample said, "I gave you five minutes. You've talked up most of it already."

Quain walked down toward the brush corral, where

the cowboys had dropped all the saddles. He picked out his and hoisted it onto his shoulder, dropping the bedroll in the process. He had to let the saddle down again to tuck part of his saddleblanket under the rope that held the bedroll together. As he disappeared into the dusk, he had the saddle over his shoulder, the bedroll under his arm, and he was looking back.

The cowboys trailed to the wagon, most of them a little shaken. They clustered around the coffeepot. Old Wash eased carefully out from behind the chuckbox, where he had stayed during the incident.

Hunter Proffitt rubbed the back of his neck and whistled between his teeth. "Isaac, you may never of had an enemy before, but you got one now."

Joe Sample said, "You oughtn't to've tried to fight him, Isaac. You ought to've let us take care of him for you."

There hadn't been time, Isaac knew. If he had waited, the only help they could have given would have been to bury him. He said, "Thanks, Mister Joe, for gettin' him off of me."

"I'd of done the same, Isaac, if I'd caught him whippin' a Bar L horse."

Isaac's shoulders slumped a little. He suspected that was true, and it somehow took away from what Joe had done for him.

Hunter Proffitt put his hand on Isaac's shoulder. "Don't you be worryin' none, Isaac. Just stick close to us; we'll take care of you."

The implication was that he could not take care of himself, and as Isaac pondered it he was not sure he actually could.

Joe Sample said, "It's against the Major's rules, but I always keep a bottle in my warbag for medicinal purposes. Right now, Isaac, you look like you could stand a dose of strong medicine." Joe went by the chuckbox and picked up a cup. He got a bottle out of his bag and poured whiskey into the cup for Isaac to drink. He crooked his finger at Wash, and the old cook came, still fearful after the violence. "Wash, Isaac took a cut on the wrist. You got somethin' in that chuckbox to fix him up with?"

Wash nodded. "Yes sir, Mister Joe, I reckon I can do that."

Isaac went to his accustomed place on the wagon-tongue, and Wash came in a minute with something brown in a bottle, and with white cloth. Hunter Proffitt and a couple of the cowboys watched with interest until Wash poured the liquid onto the long cut, then they turned quickly away. Isaac sucked a sharp breath between his teeth; it was like being touched by a white-hot iron.

Wash muttered under his breath, "That's damn little compared to what Quain'll give you if ever he gets the chanct. You gone plumb crazy, stirrin' a man up thataway?"

"Just defended myself, was all I done."

"After you'd already got him mad. Damn it, Isaac, you're six kinds of a fool. You ought to've kept your mouth shut in the beginnin', and there wouldn't of been no fight."

"He was stealin' off of the Major."

"Is that any of our business? The Major is a big rich white man; he can take care of hisownself. Ain't no need in us gittin' mixed up in white folks' business."

"The Major has always been kind to me."

"Because he always had a use for you. Get to where you ain't no use to him and see how long he's kind to you . . . see how long he even *looks* at you. Isaac, me and you, we got to take care of ourownselves. Let them white folks fight all they want to. I'm an old man, but I can outrun a good horse when trouble starts; it's somethin' I learned a long time ago."

"He wasn't no good man, that Quain. He treated me like dirt, and he stole off of the Major. He just wasn't no good man."

"But he was a *white* man. I swear, Isaac, I don't know if you'll ever live long enough for me to teach you any sense."

At the cookfire Proffitt was saying, "Did you-all see where he got cut? Under that black skin the meat was the same color as everybody else's."

The stress and the violence brought nausea to Isaac. He felt as if he would heave up his supper, and he walked out into the darkness away from the others. He stood awhile, waiting, but nothing came. The sickness stayed, however. He lay on top of his blankets, his clothes on. By ones or twos the cowboys came around to see about him, for he customarily spread his roll a little apart from the others. After a long time Isaac decided he might as well go properly to bed, so he pulled off his boots and stuck them under the blankets to protect them from dew or rain. Neither seemed very likely, but it was a good habit to cultivate. He always slept in the rest of his clothes, for he had a shift of guard duty to stand before daylight.

He lay a long time looking up at the stars, then closing his eyes and trying not to look, trying to go to sleep. The incident kept running through his mind over and over. He kept picking at the details of it, as he might restlessly pick at loose threads on an old coat. He would tell himself Wash had been right; he ought to have stayed out of other people's business. But Alvin Quain had been cheating the Major.

Or was that it? If Quain hadn't picked on Isaac and tried to humiliate and shame him, would he have given that list to Joe Sample? He didn't know; in all honesty to himself he was not at all sure he would have. Had it been one of the cowboys he liked, he knew he would not have. He had let Quain get under his skin, and that had been a damnfool thing.

He dropped off eventually into a fitful sleep, but not deep enough that he missed hearing the nightguards come in from the bobtail shift for relief at the herd. Isaac's would be the cocktail shift, the last guard before sunup. It made for a long day and a short night, but at least the night was all in one piece.

He became conscious of the sound of boots moving carefully among the bedrolls between him and the wagon. Half awake, he opened his eyes and saw the dark form of a man against the starlight. He raised up, thinking this was a rider come to get him to stand his guard.

The man said quietly, "Isaac?" and Isaac knew the voice. He saw the hand lift and knew it held a pistol. More by instinct than by thought, Isaac hurled himself to one side. The pistol fired, its single shot breaking the night stillness like a cannon blast. Barefoot, Isaac sprinted for the only cover he could think of, the chuckwagon. He felt a body stir beneath his foot and knew he had stepped on some cowboy. Not a sleeping cowboy, however; the shot had brought every man in camp instantly awake. Half a dozen men shouted in surprise and alarm.

Alvin Quain took one more wild shot at Isaac, the bullet plowing into the wagonbox. Isaac rounded the wagon in a run, his heart going like a hammer. In a moment he heard a horse running, and he knew Quain was in flight.

Joe Sample was stamping around in his underwear. "What the hell is goin' on? Who was it fired that shot?"

Isaac, trembling, came back around the chuckwagon. "It was Alvin Quain, Mister Joe. He shot at me."

Joe Sample hardly believed it at first. "Alvin Quain left here."

Not very far, Isaac thought. When he tried to put it into words, the voice wouldn't come anymore. He worked his way back to his bedroll with the idea of sitting down and getting hold of himself. He smelled something smouldering and picked up the top blanket he had flung up as he rolled out of the bed. He stuck his finger through a bullethole and found the blanket still burning at the edge of it. Quain had fired through it as it had come flying at him.

Joe Sample saw it now, and doubt left him. "I don't see how he missed you, Isaac."

Isaac found his voice. "I wasn't holdin' still."

Hunter Proffitt said, "I heard a horse runnin'. He must've caught him one after dark and come back."

Sample's fists clenched. "Then he not only tried to kill a man, but he stole a horse off of us."

Proffitt pointed. "If we get right after him, we might catch up with the snake." The cowboys, circling around, were plainly ready.

Sample shook his head. "Not in the dark; he'd lose us. We'll wait till daylight and follow his tracks. A lard-butt like him is bound to slow down sooner or later."

One of the nightherd men came loping up to see what the shooting was about. "If them steers out yonder had been a little more jumpy to start with, we'd of been chasin' them to hell and gone by now."

Isaac held out his hand and found it shaking. "Mister Joe, it's about time for my guard anyway. I'd just as well go on out."

Sample said, "No, Isaac. I imagine he'll keep runnin' this time, but if he didn't you'd be an easy target out yonder. Best you stay here."

Half a dozen cowboys who already had stood their guard volunteered to take Isaac's place; they wouldn't be going back to sleep anyway. Sample nodded to a soft-whiskered youth who had spoken first. "All right, Bud, you go."

Sample turned to find the old cook. "Wash, where you at?" Wash was on the far side of the wagon. He came out with some reluctance. Sample said, "Wash, you'd just as well get breakfast started. Everybody's up anyway."

Wash uneasily eyed first Sample, then Isaac. "Mister Joe, if that man is out yonder and we stir up this fire, we'll sure make a fancy target."

"He's after Isaac, not the rest of us. He knows he'd be hung in a minute if he was to get the wrong man." He reflected on that, looking at Isaac. "Or the right one either. You scared, Isaac?"

"You know I am."

"Don't you be. We'll either catch him or run him out of the country. We ought to've shot him when we had the chance."

Wash poked the coals to life and fed them enough chips and shavings to coax them into flame, then built up a cooking fire with larger chunks of wood. He kept looking off into the darkness as if he expected shooting to begin at any time. When he had a chance to speak to Isaac without the others hearing, he said accusingly, "See there?"

"See where?"

"See what I told you about the trouble you'd get us into? Quain is liable to come in here and kill ever one of us dead . . . me and you, anyway."

"He ain't mad at you, Wash . . . just me."

"One black face'll look the same as another to him.

Dammit, Isaac, I get in enough trouble just bein' *me*, without you bringin' me no extry."

"Like I told you before, he was robbin' the Major."

"It ain't the Major he was shootin' at, though; it was *you*. I swear, Isaac, for a full-growed man sometimes you sure ain't none too bright."

When breakfast was ready, Isaac waited his turn, then found he could not eat; his stomach felt as if he had been drinking bad water. He sipped at Wash's black coffee, which was strong enough to be something of a hazard in itself.

By the time the cowboys finished eating, daylight was pushing up over the hills, and the kid horse wrangler brought the remuda, pushing the horses through the dusty narrow gate of the brush corral. "We're missin' that dappled gray that Quain used to ride," he said to no one in particular.

Isaac picked up his bridle and walked through the gate with the rest of the cowboys, to wait for Joe Sample or Hunter Proffitt to rope out a mount for him. The two customarily did all the horse catching. Leading his own favorite dun horse at the end of the rope, Joe Sample told Isaac, "You're stayin' in camp."

Isaac was surprised, but he asked no questions.

Sample explained, "If we get close to Quain, no use givin' him another chance to shoot at you."

"Whatever you say, but I don't want to shirk my part none."

"You never have, Isaac. You stay close to the wagon and keep your eyes open."

Old Wash would have a fit, Isaac staying here with him. Isaac managed a weak smile. "It makes a man feel good, Mister Joe, to know he's got friends."

"The Big Lonesome outfit takes care of its own." Sample looked around to see if all the riders were ready. "Hunter, you and Alf Train see if you can pick up the tracks. We'll fall in behind you."

Isaac stood by the corral and watched while the two men moved out in front and began cutting back and forth, looking for sign. They were not long in finding it. In the cool morning air Isaac could hear Hunter Proffitt shout. The other riders fell in behind him, and Proffitt led them in a southerly direction, the dust hanging a long time behind them.

Isaac still had his bridle in his hand. He walked to where his saddle lay by itself on the ground, and he draped the bridle across it and the blanket, careful to keep the bits out of the dirt. He returned to the wagon, where the wrangler sat eating his belated breakfast, and where Wash stood staring in puzzlement.

Wash demanded, "How come you didn't go?"

"Joe Sample said I was to stay here and not be a target."

"You're a target here if that Quain makes up his mind to come back. And what about the rest of us that's caught here with you?"

"Mister Joe didn't figure he'll come back."

"Didn't figure it last night, either."

Isaac walked to a Dutch oven and got a half-cold biscuit. Wash backed off from him. "You stay away from me, Isaac."

Isaac was suddenly half-irritated. "You scared of me, Wash?"

"I'm scared of bein' close to you in case that crazy man comes back. It wasn't me that caused the trouble. I don't want to get shot because of what you done."

Isaac was inclined to Joe Sample's view, that Alvin Quain was unlikely to come back a second time. Bravery had never appeared to be Quain's long suit. But just the same, it would pay to be alert.

"Wash," he said, "I want that old rifle out of the chuckwagon."

Wash fetched it down and handed it to him. "Now you get away from here with it."

Isaac checked the load in it, then carried it over to the corral. He sat down with his back to the fence and settled himself for a long wait.

Chapter Four

Toward noon he saw the two horsemen, and he squinted, trying to make out who they were. He had little fear that one might be Alvin Quain; it seemed unlikely that Quain would have found a friend this quickly. Even if he had, he would not ride so boldly up to the camp. Isaac walked back to the wagon, pointing.

"Company comin', Wash."

The cook put his hand over his eyes for shade and looked apprehensively.

"Don't worry," Isaac told him, "it's not Alvin Quain."

"*You* don't know," Wash said testily. "He could be bringin' somebody."

Presently Isaac took the cartridge out of the rifle and put the weapon into the wagon. "It's the Major," he said, relieved.

Wash felt no relief. "He'll raise hell when he finds how much trouble you've caused."

Isaac made up his mind not to argue with Wash over this subject anymore. He never could win an argument with the cook anyway; the best he ever achieved was a standoff. With Wash no issue was ever dead. Old ones which Isaac had long since forgotten had a way of coming back to life with Wash when no new ones arose.

The Major was riding his favorite sorrel, a tall animal with a star face and three stocking feet. The man on the black horse was a stranger to Isaac, though it was easy to classify him as a cowboy. His clothes were well-worn, his shirt patched, his gray hat notched and pitted along the edge of the brim, an old crease in the crown pinched so many times that it had finally cracked through.

The Major lifted his hand in greeting, then swung down from the saddle, looking around camp curiously. He sensed something amiss. "How come you at the wagon this time of the day, Isaac? How come I don't see cattle gathered, except the steer herd?"

Wash didn't give Isaac time to frame an answer. "They're all out chasin' after Alvin Quain, Major," Wash put in quickly. "He taken a shot at Isaac last night."

The stranger studied Isaac a moment, his eyes not friendly. "Is that all?"

Wash said, "He stole a horse, too."

The stranger nodded. "Well then, that makes more sense."

The Major gave Isaac a worried scrutiny. "Shot at you, Isaac? Did he hit you?"

"No sir, he missed."

The stranger, still on horseback, said dryly, "I reckon he *would* be a little hard to see in the dark. You didn't tell me this was a black outfit, Major."

The Major frowned but otherwise ignored the comment. "Quain wasn't any prize, but I don't expect he shot at you without some sort of cause. What was the trouble, Isaac?"

Isaac told him as briefly as he could about the trip to town, about Quain adding items to the chuck list and then evidently swapping them off at Big Bessie's.

The Major cursed under his breath. "World's coming to a pretty pass. If I don't get robbed on a dark street, I get robbed at my own chuckwagon. It's enough to test a man's faith in humanity."

The stranger got down from the saddle. "What're you doin' *with* a faith in humanity, Major? I lost mine a long time ago."

"What *do* you have faith in, Pete?"

"Myself, and one or two good horses I've known. I distrust everything and everybody else."

"Including me?"

The stranger shrugged. "Like I said, you didn't tell me this was a black outfit."

"It's not, except for Isaac and Wash here. Don't let their complexion fool you. Wash can cook as good a meal as ever you ate, and you'll ride a long time hunting for a better all-around cowboy than Isaac."

The stranger grunted.

The Major introduced him as Pete Runyan. The cowboy made no move to shake hands, so Isaac didn't either. He had learned from boyhood that some white men had a feeling about that, so he never pushed.

"If you're so good," Runyan said, "how come you're standin' around here instead of bein' out yonder with the rest of them huntin' that *hombre*?"

"Joe Sample told me to stay here. Whatever the wagon-boss tells me, I do it."

"Well," Runyan said to the Major, "there's that much to be said for him; he takes orders. I'll bet he didn't mind this one none."

Isaac's teeth ground together. He decided he wasn't going to like Pete Runyan any better than he had liked Alvin Quain.

The Major walked to Wash's coffeepot but found the coffee not ready yet. Wash had not put it over the coals until he had seen the Major coming. "You brought the ponies that I bought over at Dry Wells?"

Isaac told him he had. The Major asked what he had thought of them. Isaac said, "All right, most of them. They'll pitch a right smart at first."

"A pitching horse never hurt a man as long as he stayed in the saddle," the Major observed. "Looks like the day is lost anyhow, as far as getting any cow work done is concerned. Take my horse, Isaac, and you and Pete run out to the remuda and bring up those ponies. We'd just as well be trying them out as sitting around the wagon doing nothing."

Isaac knew only too well who the Major meant by *we*, for the Major never rode any broncs himself. He said, "Yes sir," and swung into the saddle. The Major's stirrups were a little short for him, bringing his knees up uncomfortably high, but he guessed he wouldn't keep the Major waiting by taking time to change over to his own saddle.

Moving along in a trot, he sensed that Pete Runyan

was studying him critically, and he knew he looked a little ridiculous in this saddle that didn't fit his legs. *But what the hell?* he thought with a tug of resentment. *He doesn't like me anyway. I won't worry myself over what he thinks.*

The horse wrangler was a cotton-headed, freckled kid of fifteen nicknamed Beau. His clothes were ragged and his old boots scarred and run over at the heels, and his face seemed always peeling from sunburn. He sat on the ground, slouched in the shadow of his horse where he could keep a watch of sorts over the scattered, grazing remuda. Isaac and Runyan rode upon him before he realized he was not alone. He looked around, startled because he saw Runyan first and did not know him.

"I swear, Isaac, you sure do look funny with your legs up like that. How come you're ridin' the Major's horse?"

Runyan gave Isaac no time for an answer. He said critically, "You'd of looked funny if we'd been a pair of Indians."

"Ain't no Indians left in this country."

"I understand somebody stole one of your horses. I can see now how you went and let it happen."

Defensively Beau said, "I wasn't asleep last night."

"I'd hate to bet on it. You was sure asleep just now."

Beau turned to Isaac, letting all his anger show. "Who is this bigmouth, Isaac? Is he somebody I got to say 'yes sir' to, or can I tell him to go to hell?"

Isaac shrugged. "Major just said his name is Pete Runyan. Didn't say nothin' else."

Beau demanded, "You some kind of a damned new strawboss or somethin', Runyan? 'Cause if you are, I'm sure as hell leavin'."

Runyan stared him down. "You're a way too young to be throwin' cusswords around like that. Careful with them or somebody'll have to blister your south end with a leather strap."

Beau's face flamed, and he took a swing at Runyan's jaw. Runyan jerked his head back a little to be sure Beau missed, then stuck his foot out and tripped the kid. Beau went down so hard on his stomach that he lost most of his breath.

Isaac quickly stepped forward to help him up.

Runyan said, "Leave him alone, boy."

Isaac ignored Runyan and got Beau to his feet. Gasping for breath, Beau made as if to go after Runyan again. Isaac held onto him. "Easy, Beau, he's baitin' you."

Runyan grunted. "I wasn't baitin' him. I just always been one to say what's true."

Isaac held onto Beau until he could see that the boy's anger had run out a little. Beau regained his breath and demanded, "What about him, Isaac? Has he got any authority over us, or anything?"

Isaac shrugged. "Major didn't say one way or the other."

Runyan shook his head. "I just hired on here as a cowboy, like everybody else."

Beau retorted, "Not like everybody. I'm glad to say there ain't anybody else in this outfit like *you*. You go messin' around with *me* anymore and you'll wish you'd taken you a dose of salts instead."

Runyan stared at him coolly. "Boy, did you ever see a cottontail rabbit jump on a lobo wolf?"

Beau shook his head, and Runyan added, "The cottontail is too smart for that. I hope you got as much sense as a rabbit." He turned to Isaac. "You got anything to say?"

Isaac said, "I reckon not."

"All right then, let's cut out them ponies the Major wants rode."

They were fairly easy to pick within the remuda, for they were still mostly to themselves in bunches of three or four, scattered among the others; the rest of the horses had not yet fully accepted the newcomers and had a tendency to keep them isolated. Older horses, in particular, obliged the young ones to keep their distance, showing no tolerance for youthful foolishness. The wrangler and Pete Runyan kept the other horses from scattering too much while Isaac went in and picked up the broncs. When he had them all thrown out from the rest, he saw Runyan coming to help him take them to the pens. He heard Beau call after Runyan, "I hope you get your smart-aleck tail busted."

Isaac smiled to himself and turned so Runyan wouldn't see his face. Beau had expressed his own wishes perfectly.

He got the broncs lined out in the right direction, then loped up near the lead to keep them pointed that way. If there was any dust to be eaten, he would let Pete Runyan eat it. There were ways, when a man knew them and did not overplay his hand, to take a dozen minor forms of revenge. Isaac had long since learned to accept his satisfaction in small doses.

A brush wing had been built out from the corral gate as an aid to hazing the animals through the opening, and Isaac loped ahead to block off the end of the wing. He shouted and waved his arm, and the broncs went in just as they were supposed to. Runyan rode on through the gate but made no move to dismount and close it; he left that chore for Isaac. Isaac stepped off his horse, tying it outside, then swung the gate, holding it just wide enough for Major Lytton to come through afoot. He shut and fastened it.

Pete Runyan studied the broncs, which had gone to the far side of the pen and now trotted in a circle through the swirling dust, warily eyeing the men. Runyan took the coiled rope from his saddlehorn and handed his reins to Isaac to hold.

Looks like he's already took over, Isaac thought.

Runyan asked the Major, "They ever been rode?"

"Horse trader told me they'd each had one or two saddles is all. They've been staked out a time or two to learn about the hackamore. Other than that, they're as green as grass."

"Probably better anyway. At least they ain't had a chance to be spoiled by somebody that don't know what he's doin'." Runyan glanced back at Isaac. "Take the saddle off my horse for me. We'd just as well find out what they're made of."

While Isaac slipped the saddle off and dropped it to the ground, Runyan shook out a big horse loop and moved patiently forward, trying not to booger the broncs. Most of them trotted restlessly back and forth up and down the far end of the pen, but two or three stood facing him, ears pointed forward. He had their undivided attention. He talked softly as he moved up, his right hand crossed over about even with his left shoulder, holding the loop up so that the tip of it barely missed dragging the ground.

The hand moved, building momentum as he brought the loop back in front of him, then up and over in a backhand twist, sailing outward and settling over the head of a Mexican-looking brown horse before it could duck out of the way. Runyan jerked the slack out of the loop, and the bronc was caught. Its eyes opened wide, and it squealed in surprise as the rope closed around its neck. It began to rear and plunge.

A little grudgingly, Isaac admitted to himself that Runyan knew how to handle that loop. He watched the cowboy gradually work his way up the rope to the bronc, and he could tell that this was by no means the first time Runyan had ever done that, either.

Runyan glanced back over his shoulder at Isaac and shouted, "Don't stand there suckin' your thumb; bring me a hackamore!"

Isaac was still holding Runyan's horse, so he did not push himself overly hard leading the animal to a fence where he could tie it. The Major had brought a couple of hackamores out from the wagon. Instead of taking one to Runyan himself, he waited and let Isaac do it. Isaac took no offense; the Major paid wages so he didn't have to do menial things like that for himself.

Isaac worked up the rope past Runyan and was about to try putting the hackamore on the brown bronc. Runyan said crisply, "What do you think you're doin'? You hold this rope and *I'll* hackamore him."

Isaac stepped back, hoping things might take a turn for the better and the bronc would get both forefeet in Runyan's shirt pocket. But it didn't. Runyan boldly put his right arm over the pony's neck and threw his body in close so that the pawing forefeet couldn't touch him. In a minute he had the hackamore on the pony's head and had slipped the rope off its neck. Now he held the bronc by the strong rope rein platted in to fit beneath the jaw. He motioned for Isaac to take the rein. "Hold him, boy."

Runyan coiled his rope, shook out a small loop, and caught one of the bronc's forefeet. In a minute he had the foot lashed up, the rope securely tied around the horse's neck so that the animal could not get the foot down. The bronc tried to hop around on three feet, went down once and threshed a moment, then got back onto three feet again, trembling a little.

"Now, son," Runyan spoke gently, "time you got to know about a saddleblanket."

He picked up the blanket and held it forward so the bronc could get a good look at it. Then, moving slowly, careful not to do anything sudden, he brought the blanket up and let it fall onto the pony's back. The bronc jumped. Runyan never quite turned loose of the blanket, and as it would start to slip he would pull it free and throw it back into place again. Gradually the bronc became reconciled to the feel of it across its back, though it would be a long time before all the reaction was gone.

"And now," Runyan said presently, "let's see how you like the saddle."

The bronc did not care for it very much, and the first time it managed, even on three feet, to jump out from under the rig. Runyan could not manage to hold onto it, and it fell to the ground, the stirrups popping against one another.

Runyan glared at Isaac. "Hold him a little tighter, boy," and he picked up the saddle to try again. Isaac's cut wrist hurt a little, but he tried not to give in to it. After a few times the pony quit crow-hopping out from under the saddle. Runyan stepped up close, reached under to grab the girth buckle, and cinched the saddle down as best he could. The bronc, walling its eyes and trying to look back at him, had a hump in its spine that made the rear of the saddle stand up.

"I'll take the rein now," Runyan said to Isaac. "I'll want you to ear him down for me." Runyan tied the free end of the rein under the hackamore to form a loop. Isaac untied the rope to let the forefoot down, letting the pony kick free. Then he grabbed both ears and held tight while Runyan got his left foot in the stirrup and swung up into the saddle.

"Stand clear," Runyan told him, and Isaac jumped away.

The bronc bawled in fear at the feel of the man on

its back, answering some ancient instinct inherited through generations of ancestors which had bucked and pitched to throw off attacking predators. It began jumping, plunging, bawling.

Throw him off! Isaac wanted to shout, but he kept his silence. Excitement built in him as he watched the bronc pitch across the pen, scattering the other horses like quail before a dog. *Dump him flat on his belly!*

The Major said, "Shame on you, Isaac."

Isaac glanced at him and saw the man smiling. "I didn't say nothin', Major. Does it show all that much?"

"It shows. You have to work at it to get to like Pete Runyan."

"He does fancy himself a right smart. I reckon he likes himself enough that he don't really need nobody else to do it."

"At least he doesn't come here under any false pretenses. He knows how to ride that bronc."

Isaac shrugged. "I expect most any man in this camp could ride that brown horse, Major. It ain't half as tough as it looks."

The horse pitched itself down and finally stood quivering, exhausted, fearful. Runyan patted it on the neck, which made it shy and try weakly to jump again, but it no longer had the strength. Runyan talked easily to the animal and kept patting it, and gradually it eased a little. Runyan grasped the horn with his right hand, reached forward and grasped both mane and rein in the left, then swung quickly to the ground. The pony shied away a step, but Runyan kept talking, moving up the rein and then touching the animal gently on the neck, rubbing a little, moving his hand up the neck and down the face to the nose, letting the horse get the feel of his hand, letting it know there was no harm in the man.

Presently he turned to Isaac. "See there, black boy? All it takes is the knowin' how. Even you could do it if you worked at it long enough."

Isaac gritted his teeth and simply nodded.

Runyan said, "We'll stake this one outside and catch us another. I want the Major to get his money's worth."

Half under his breath, Isaac said, "The Major always gets his money's worth, sooner or later."

He helped Runyan unsaddle the brown, then led the animal outside while it rolled its eyes and resisted the rein. He tied it to the fence, where it could fight against the hackamore and the rein with the same determination as it had initially fought against Runyan, and with the same negative results. In time the horse would learn a healthy respect for the rein, and learn to obey its gentlest commands.

While Isaac was taking care of that, Runyan was roping a second bronc. They went through the same motions with this one, tying up one forefoot while they saddled it, sacking it out and putting the saddle on its back, then sliding it off a few times. Before long Runyan was on it; it was pitching with him just as the brown had done, and Runyan was riding it with almost a lazy ease.

Isaac watched him with eyes narrowed. *Just you wait, smart britches, till you try that bay.*

The bay was the fourth bronc Runyan caught. Isaac could tell from the moment the rope sailed around the bronc's neck that this was going to be different from the others; this was going to be hell on a handcar. The bay did not wait for the blanket or the saddle. It pitched and bawled and kicked and fought at the rope. Runyan simply held onto the rope and let the bronc have its way for a while, expecting it to wear itself down. It showed little sign of that, however. In time Runyan passed the rope on to Isaac and took a second rope, with which he caught the bay's forefeet. He jerked up the slack, then brought the rope around his waist and jabbed his bootheels hard against the ground, letting his body take the impact as the bronc hit the end of the rope. The horse went down hard, kicking, threshing, squealing, then was up again, pitching and pawing, throwing the rope off. Runyan roped the forefeet once more and sent the bronc crashing, knocking some of the breath out of it this time.

In the moment the horse was stunned, Runyan rushed forward and began the process of tying up a forefoot as he had done with the others. With Isaac's help he eventually got the job done, but when he had the foot tied the bronc was nowhere near giving up. It crow-hopped on the other three feet, squealing at this outrage, pawing futilely at the man who had treated him so roughly.

Sweat soaked the back of Runyan's shirt, and under his arms. Dust lay thick on his face, streaked into little patterns of mud by beads of perspiration which rolled down his cheeks and down his neck and disappeared into his open collar. He was breathing hard now, tiring. No one would have blamed him if he had quit here and left the bay for another day, but Runyan gave no sign he even considered it. He stood his ground and advanced up the rope and fought the hackamore into place while the bay tried wickedly to paw and bite. Those hoofs struck him a couple of blows that Isaac knew must have hurt. But Runyan never faltered or looked as if he wanted to quit.

He sacked out the bay as he had done the others, and swung the saddle up and pulled it off repeatedly. The horse never stopped fighting him. Runyan eventually got the saddle cinched down as tightly as he could, though the hump in the bay's back made the saddle appear to stand up almost on end. Isaac pulled the slip knot in the rope that held the forefoot, then grabbed both ears and held tight while Runyan swung quickly into the saddle.

"Let him go!" Runyan shouted, and Isaac was more than glad to. He jumped clear, seeing out of the corner of his eye that he had narrowly missed being pawed by a forefoot. Isaac half fell in his haste to get away, catching a mouthful of dust, turning as he pushed up from one knee. He saw the bronc go straight up, eyes wide, mouth open, teeth seeming to flash. He heard the scream that was half fear, half fury as the bay reacted to the grip of the saddle, to the weight of the man on its back. He heard the pop of leather, the grunt of the rider, the great slosh of water in the bronc's belly. The dust churned, the hoofs pounded. Isaac scrambled to get farther in the clear, for in its blind anxiety to rid itself of the man, this bronc would kick, stomp, or run over anything that chanced into its path.

For a moment Isaac thought Runyan was going to ride him, and he felt a grudging admiration for the man's courage. But daylight winked between man and saddle, and a stirrup flopped free. Isaac backed off a couple more steps to be sure Runyan didn't land on top of him.

Runyan came down on his side with a thump like a sack of cornmeal dropped off a wagon. He rolled over, scrambling to get away from those slashing hoofs.

The bay seemed not to know at first that it had rid itself of the man, for the saddle was still there, and the stirrups flopped up and down, popping against each other, against the saddle, against the horse's sides. Pete Runyan pushed up onto hands and knees and peered through the dust, confused for a moment, then angry as his vision cleared.

"Catch him, Goddammit!"

Catching the bay was almost as tough an order as riding him had been. Three times Isaac got hold of the reins, then lost them before he managed to get a firm hold and keep it.

"Ear him down," Runyan wheezed.

As Isaac held the squealing bronc, Runyan swung into the saddle and once more ordered Isaac to stand clear. Again, it looked for a few seconds as if Runyan was going to fit a ride on him. He kept a good seat the first several jumps. But Isaac could see from the ground that this bay had a peculiar twist that threw Runyan off balance. Runyan came down hard, striking on his shoulder and rolling over, again moving quickly to get out of the way. It was well he did, for the bay pitched over the spot where Runyan had landed, kicking up clods of dirt.

Major Lytton came forward. He studied Runyan critically as the cowboy pushed himself up from the ground. "You're tired out, Runyan. Quit before he really hurts you."

Runyan stubbornly shook his head and felt around on the ground for his fallen hat. He had taken such a pounding that he could not see straight. "I never like to turn one loose till I've rode him. Let one get away with throwin' you, it spoils him. Go catch him for me, boy."

Isaac eared the bay down a third time while Runyan got on, slower now. Isaac stepped out of the way and turned to watch. If the bronc had slowed any, it was not evident to the eye. It was as violent this time as it had been before. Runyan lasted three jumps and came down on his stomach. He lay there gasping, trying to regain his breath.

Major Lytton said, "That's enough. Isaac, unsaddle that bronc."

Runyan seemed inclined to argue about it, but he lacked the breath. Isaac managed to worry the saddle off, the bronc kicking it mightily as it hit the ground. Isaac got the bronc over to a fence and took two quick wraps around a post. He tied a half hitch and stood back to let the horse fight a futile battle against the hackamore, the heavy rein, and the stout post.

Runyan was on hands and knees, breathing hard. His hat lay halfway across the corral, mashed flat. "Major . . . ," he wheezed, "that bay . . . that bay is pure hell. I got a notion . . . there ain't no man . . . ever goin' to ride him."

The Major glanced at Isaac. "Let's help Runyan out of here."

Runyan shook his head, waving them away. He pushed to his feet, going deep for breath. He looked at the bronc, struggling against the hackamore rein. "Son-of-a-bitch, he ain't whipped me yet."

Chapter Five

Pete Runyan took a long rest at the wagon, cradling a cup of Wash's black coffee between his hands while he sat on the thin roll of blankets he had brought tied behind the high cantle of his saddle.

Good thing it's still warm weather, Isaac thought. *No more sugans than that, he'd take his death of chill in a cold time.* It was custom for two men to pool their blankets and share the thicker roll. Isaac was glad he wouldn't be asked. Here across the fire was as close as he cared to get to Runyan.

While he rested, Runyan's eyes were on the corral, and specifically on that bay bronc.

Wash shuffled over from the chuckbox with a heavy cloth in his hand, picked up the hot coffeepot from its place on the coals, and carried it to Runyan. All smiles and white teeth he said, "You like another cup, Mister Runyan?"

Runyan shook his head. "Damned bronc like to've killed me. I expect your coffee would just about finish the job."

Old Wash stood and blinked, hurt. Some people were not overly fond of his sourdough biscuits, and others didn't think much of the rocks he sometimes left in the beans, but nobody ever complained about his coffee. Major Lytton said, "I'll take some more, Wash."

Runyan glanced reprovingly at the Major, as a parent might at someone who sympathizes with his just-disciplined child. But Runyan said nothing. Instead he looked at Isaac. "Boy, you about rested up enough to tackle some more of them broncs?"

Isaac shrugged. "*I* never was tired."

The man's stamina amazed Isaac, though he was sure he could have done the same thing himself had he needed to. Before Joe Sample and the cowboys came in, Runyan had taken a seat on every bronc in the corral. He had not given any of them a long ride, but enough to see what kind of fight they showed, and to make his own estimation of their eventual worth.

"That little sorrel," he pointed for the Major, "is liable to be the best horse in the bunch. If you ain't got him in mind for somebody else, I'd be tickled to have him in my string. That little U-necked brown ain't going to be fit for much, unless you want to give him to the horse wrangler, or to this boy here." Runyan jerked his head at Isaac.

A touch of humor came into the Major's eyes. Isaac had an idea the Major was somehow perversely enjoying this. The Major said, "Maybe I'll give him to the wrangler."

Runyan shrugged. "Do as you think best."

The Major said, "I always do."

Sample and the cowboys trailed back late in the afternoon, some straggling two hundred yards behind the others on tired horses. Their silence made it plain they had not succeeded. The cowboys stepped down outside the corral and slipped the saddles off their horses. Joe Sample acknowledged the Major's arrival by riding over to the wagon where the ranch owner stood. "Didn't know when you was comin', Major. Glad you're back." He glanced at the broncs in the corral, then gave Pete Runyan a moment of quiet study but asked no questions. It was customary in range country to wait and see how much information was volunteered.

The Major said, "I take it you didn't find Alvin Quain."

"We had his tracks for a ways, but he lost us when we got over in them breaks to the south." Sample looked at the black cowboy. "Sorry, Isaac."

The Major shrugged. "Well, I reckon he's gone

py-yi." That was an Anglo cowboy corruption of a Mexican term that meant *over yonder* or *plumb gone.*

Joe Sample frowned. "I hope so. I'd hate to think of him slippin' back into camp at night. . . ." He looked at Isaac and left the rest unsaid.

The Major shook his head. "He'd have to hate Isaac awfully bad; I don't see how he could figure it was worth it."

"Isaac had to lay hands on him, Major. There's some men would take that like a mortal wound."

The Major took a long look at Isaac. "That being the case," he said grimly, "tell the boys that if they ever see Quain on Bar L range they'd better shoot him. He stole a horse; that ought to satisfy the law."

Pete Runyan had listened quietly. Now he protested. "You'd kill a man just because he hates some crow? Hell, you'd have to kill half the men from the Mississippi to the Pecos River."

The Major said, "Not for hating, but for hating badly enough to do murder."

"I'd wait to see if he really *did* murder before I opened the season on him."

Stiffly Joe Sample declared, "That wouldn't do Isaac much good."

Runyan plainly wasn't concerned about that. "If Isaac don't like his chances here, they tell me they like his kind out in California."

Sample's face colored. He took a step toward Runyan. "We sort of like ol' Isaac right here. And who the hell are *you* in the first place?"

The Major spoke up. "Stand easy, Joe. This is Pete Runyan. He saved me from being robbed the other night. I hired him."

Sample backed off the step he had taken. "Hired him? Well, I hope there's somethin' he can do besides work his jaw."

The Major jerked his thumb toward the corral. "He topped off all those new broncs."

Sample half-turned, looking at the broncs staked to the fence and the others still loose in the corral because there had not been enough hackamores. "Every one of them?"

"Every one of them."

"And he *rode* them?"

Runyan said matter-of-factly, "Every one. Well, all but one; there's one in there that there ain't nobody can ride."

Sample knew immediately. "The bay."

Hunter Proffitt was walking up from the corral, where he had turned his horse loose outside. Sample called to him, "Hunter, I wisht you'd take a turn at that bay bronc in yonder. This feller says there ain't nobody on this ranch can ride him."

Proffitt gave Pete Runyan a long *go-to-hell* study and said, "Sure, Joe. Won't be no trouble atall."

It was a great deal of trouble. It took Proffitt some time simply to get his saddle on the bronc's back. It took far less time for the bay to send Proffitt sailing like a bird on the wing. Proffitt got up using hard language and swung into the saddle again while a couple of the cowboys held the bay for him. This time he landed so hard that he lay gasping for air as the bronc pitched squealing across the corral, the loose stirrups flopping and popping. Two of the cowboys had to get Proffitt's arms up and over their shoulders and half carry him outside.

Isaac and Joe Sample rushed to see if Proffitt was hurt. The breath had been knocked out of him. Isaac pounded his hand against Proffitt's back, trying to start him breathing again.

The Major looked through the brush fence at the bronc, which still pitched, trying to rid itself of the saddle. "Maybe I *had* better get rid of that bay before he kills somebody."

Pete Runyan smiled in satisfaction. "Don't, Major."

"You said yourself that I ought to."

"I've changed my mind. I'm goin' to keep after that bay till I show these fair-weather cowboys of yours how a *man* rides a bronc."

Some of the cowboys muttered resentfully, and Hunter Proffitt glared in mute helplessness, still gasping.

Right then, Isaac figured, Pete Runyan lost any chance he might have had to cultivate friends in this camp. But Runyan showed no sign that he gave a damn, and Isaac suspected he did not.

The cattle work went about normally from then on.
Each day the unbranded calves were roped out of the
herd and dragged up close to the fire for their sudden
acquaintance with the hot iron. The long-age steers,
mostly three- and four-year-olds, were cut out of the
bunch and loose-herded to themselves. Every three or
four days, when this steer herd was big enough to justify
the job, a few cowboys would be dispatched to drive it
down to the south part of the ranch to be turned loose
with other steers gathered earlier. When the branding
was done it would be time to gather these steers and
drive them to the place where buyer Lon Whitten would
pick them up. Then, cash in hand, the Major could make
his annual payment to the bank and thumb his nose once
again at Fort Worth banker J. Warren Norris, who
waited like a vulture on a dead cottonwood limb to
swoop down and eat up the luckless.

After supper the first few days, each cowboy would
catch out the new bronc assigned to him and throw a
saddle on it, then climb up for a session of court. Some
had more luck than others. When a cowboy was thrown
for the second time, Pete Runyan was always there like a
handful of salt thrown in a wound. Having already
topped out the sorrel he had taken for himself, he was
ready and willing to take over any bronc that someone
else could not ride. He would sit in that high-pitching
saddle with an ease and an arrogance that soon had every
man in camp hating him. He would ride the bronc until it
was too tired to put up much fight, then turn it back to
the man who had been thrown and tell him, "Now
maybe even you can ride him."

Isaac did not get one of the new broncs, so he was
principally a spectator at these sessions, except that he
would help ear down a horse which needed it, or hold
the rope while someone else did.

Runyan's superiority extended not only to the bronc
stomping but to the branding sessions as well. Hunter
Proffitt took particular pride in his ability as a heeler; he
would ride into the herd, rope an unbranded calf by its
heels, and drag it out to the fire. A calf caught by the
heels was far easier on the flanking crew because it could

not put up as much fight as one caught around the neck. Heeling was a special art, just as roping horses out of the remuda was a talent given to few. Many a cowpuncher otherwise handy with a loop could never quite master this specialty.

Hunter usually took the heeling as his own particular job because he was more skilled at it than anyone else in camp. He usually made two catches out of three tries, dragging the cattle out on a big strong gray horse.

But the third day after Pete Runyan's arrival, Hunter Proffitt was somehow off stride. He was missing half or more of his loops, and the pairs of flankers near the fire beyond the edge of the herd often stood around with nothing to do, waiting for him.

Pete Runyan was flanking calves in partnership with steady, one-eyed Alf Train. Hunter Proffitt came out, his big gray horse straining against the weight of a long-age calf at the end of the rope. A pair of flankers pounced on the bawling calf and laid it over on its side, ready for iron and knife. Proffitt swung down, sweating hard, and proceeded to tighten his cinch. Pete Runyan said, "I'll take it awhile and give these flankers somethin' to do. You go get yourself a cigarette."

Proffitt backed away, too surprised to offer resistance. He got hold of himself and shouted angrily, "You bring that horse back here!" But Runyan was already in the herd.

He made it look so easy it was almost shameful. His loop would make a couple of quick little swings and dart to the ground, picking up a calf's heels. Runyan would jerk up the slack to secure the loop, then touch spurs to the gray's ribs and come out in a hard trot, jerking the calf down hard enough to knock some of the fight out of it.

It didn't take him long to catch up to the flanking crews. Then he got ahead of them, catching calves so fast that he often had to wait till a pair of flankers could turn loose of a finished calf and be ready to tackle the latest one he had dragged up.

Isaac handled the branding irons, keeping wood fed to the fire, and the hot coals spread broadly enough that each used iron soon came back to a red glow. It was hot, sweaty work. Runyan's quick skill with the rope kept Isaac in a trot much of the time. Runyan dragged calves up about as rapidly as Isaac could brand them.

Isaac felt the resentment of the flanking crews. He pushed harder to get the branding done and enable the men to let the calves up quicker. It became a grim, silent contest—Runyan alone on one side, everybody else against him. Isaac tried for an hour to be fast enough to let the crews just once get ahead of Runyan.

Hunter Proffitt had teamed with Alf Train in flanking, and the two men worked with the precision of a good watch, trying—as Isaac tried—to get ahead of Runyan. They never made it. Proffitt muttered as Isaac pressed a hot iron against a speckled hide and acrid yellow smoke curled up from the burning hair. "He's showin' off, is all he's doin'. He's makin' like he's better than the rest of us."

Train grunted. "Hell, Hunter, he *is* better than the rest of us. That's what makes him so damned hard to take."

"Sooner or later," Proffitt gritted, "somebody is goin' to land him flat on his butt. And it's as apt to be me as anybody."

The only satisfaction the cowboys had was in the bay bronc. Every evening when the other work was done, Runyan would saddle the bay. He no longer had to tie up a foot. The bronc would let him put the saddle on, almost as if it welcomed the contest. It always ended the same way: Runyan going down. Runyan would usually take two falls . . . occasionally three . . . then quit for the evening. But though the cowboys hollered for the bronc and took satisfaction when Runyan fell, their victory was always short of being complete. Runyan never gave up; they knew he would tackle that bay again.

Pete Runyan soon preempted Hunter Proffitt's unquestioned position as number-one heeler when the calves were branded, and before long he was roping horses out of the remuda when it came time for the men to change mounts. His speed with the rope outshone even Joe Sample, who had long been acknowledged as the best man in the country with a horse loop.

But whatever inner victory Runyan won by competing hard and beating everyone else he paid for in ostracism. At mealtime there were always two men sitting alone on wagontongues, black Isaac Jefford at his accustomed place near the front of the chuckwagon, Pete Runyan across at the hoodlum wagon, taking his meal in silence, an exile of sorts. But it was an exile of his own choice and making.

Isaac wondered sometimes why the Major did not do something to stop this angry rivalry. But the Major usually ignored it, and when he could not ignore it he seemed to take a perverse enjoyment from it. It had brought the Major some gain. Every man was putting out his best, working faster and harder under the bitter spur of Pete Runyan's insolent superiority. Isaac wondered how the Major would smile if this thing led to a killing.

They finished the branding, and it was time to round up the big steers from the south part of the ranch where they had been driven afoot in small bunches. That took several days, for some had strayed back toward the ranges they were accustomed to grazing. When the job was done, Major Estel Lytton had well over a thousand steers ready to drive to Dry Wells for delivery to Lon Whitten on the appointed day when Whitten was to arrive with his drovers.

Whitten customarily bought them from the Major on speculation, as he bought many other herds around the country, driving them north to the railroad in hope he could resell at a profit. The Major had always considered ranching to be gamble enough in itself; he preferred to take his profit on his own home ground, if there *was* a profit. He knew of too many cattlemen who had been fed to the financial wolves when they reached the railroad and found the buyers in collusion to beat the price down.

The morning they started the drive, Pete Runyan asked no one. He simply rode out and assumed the right point position for himself. The point had always been Hunter Proffitt's place. Hunter glanced back in anger at the Major. The Major said blandly, "Hunter, I'd be obliged if you'd take the swing." Hunter rode off talking under his breath in words not quite intelligible, but a blind mule would have understood the meaning.

By this time all the broncs Isaac had brought from town had been broken enough that they were in regular use . . . all but that bay. Joe Sample had told the kid wrangler when they pulled out of ranch headquarters to leave the bay behind, but Pete Runyan had cut the bay back into the remuda. Joe had watched quietly. When the wrangler looked to Joe for orders, Joe had simply shrugged and turned away.

The first day's drive was made hard and fast, purposely tiring the steers so they would be less likely to want to run that night. To make a run even less likely, a set of brush corrals had been built at the point where the Lytton drives always camped on their first night. The cattle were watered in a creek, then pushed into the pens to bed down.

That done and supper finished, Pete Runyan rode out to the remuda, dropped a loop around the bay's neck, and led the bronc back to a small brush corral not being used for the cattle. As he rode near the chuckwagon he crooked a finger at Isaac. "Come on, boy, you're goin' to help me."

Isaac pushed to his feet. Hunter Proffitt growled, "See if you can cut his cinch, Isaac. Maybe that bay'll finally bust his neck."

It had been two or three days since Runyan had had time to try the bronc. It was rested up and ready to fight. It took a notion it didn't want the saddle, and it squealed and pawed and pitched out from under both blanket and saddle two or three times while Isaac held grimly to the hackamore and reins.

"Get in there tight against him and hold him up!" Runyan ordered angrily. "Bite down on his ear. I swear, I never saw a black boy yet that wasn't scared of a horse."

Angered, Isaac was tempted to turn the bronc loose and let Runyan see what he could do by himself. But he took a tighter grip and got close like Runyan said. In a minute Runyan had the saddle on and cinched up as tight as the hump in the bay's back would permit. Runyan got hold of the hackamore rein and swung up while Isaac held the horse's ears. He heard Runyan say, "All right, bay horse, this is the time. I'm goin' to ride you or kill you!" To Isaac, Runyan shouted, "Now turn him loose and get your lazy carcass out of the way!"

Isaac stepped aside. The bay went by him like a steaming locomotive. The horse ran two or three lengths, then went straight up, bawling. Coming down, it broke wind and gave a hard twist that snapped Runyan's head around. It landed hard and went straight up again, squealing, mouth open, teeth bared. This time the twist was different, and Runyan shifted abruptly to one side. Isaac could hear the hard thump of impact as the horse hit the ground and the man's rump slammed against the saddle.

The third jump did not lose Runyan entirely, but it was plain to see he would not stay up much longer. He had lost control, hitting the pommel of the saddle one time, the horn the next. But he kept spurring, kept cursing.

In its rage the bronc slammed into the brush fence, breaking through and coming down astraddle it. Runyan was down on the bronc's side, pinned helplessly between the saddle and the broken fence while the animal threshed wildly for solid ground. Isaac saw that Runyan's ribs could be smashed as the fence had been smashed.

Runyan cried out, "Help me! Get him off of me!"

The horse kept fighting while Isaac stood there, frozen a moment in surprise, unable to get himself moving. He heard Runyan cry out in pain, heard the dry brush crackling. Then Isaac ran to the struggling horse and grabbed the big hackamore rein. Runyan was on the far side, pinned; the only way Isaac could help him would be to get the horse up. He could see Runyan's anxious face, drained from pain and fear.

Isaac pulled, trying to get the horse free of the fence, free of Runyan. A hind foot lashed, and it struck something solid. Isaac hoped it was only the fence.

He pulled hard, and both of the horse's forefeet somehow touched the ground. The bay gave a lunge and freed itself. It pitched a jump, its feet back on the solid ground. Isaac held on to the reins.

Runyan lay in the shattered fence, eyes wide in

shock. He began to curse Isaac. "You lazy black son-of-a-bitch, what makes you so damned slow?"

Isaac decided then that Runyan wasn't really hurt. He was probably bruised a solid blue, but the impact had not jarred the meanness out of him. Isaac wished he had left the horse alone a moment longer.

Runyan struggled to work free, cursing all the while. "Never was one of you crows could do anything right."

Anger washed over Isaac in a flood. He had taken Runyan's insults as long as he could. A dozen times he might have hit him with his fist, but he had held himself back. Now he was going to hit him in another way, even harder.

Isaac shoved his left foot into the stirrup and swung quickly up into the saddle, throwing his weight a little forward to offset the bay's quick lunge. He barely got his right foot into its stirrup before the bay bawled and took that first jump straight up. Isaac had time for just a glimpse of Runyan pushing up out of the fence, staring in amazement. Then he set himself for that wicked twist he had seen this bronc use so many times. It came, and he weathered it, as he weathered the sudden impact of the bronc hitting the ground forefeet first, then the hind feet. The bronc went up again, twisting another direction as he came down.

But Isaac had a grip on him, and he had a grip on himself. He was not fighting the horse now, he was fighting Pete Runyan. He was determined that no matter what this bay bronc did it was not going to shake Isaac Jefford.

And it didn't. A time or two Isaac felt himself weakening, but he managed to take a deeper hold. The bronc pitched around and around the corral, bawling in frustration, trying every variation on that wicked twist, while Isaac stuck like a burr on a blanket. Gradually Isaac felt the bay tiring beneath him. He felt safe and a little brave, and he began to make a show of it, shouting, waving his hat, using the spurs.

Things were moving too fast for him to see very well what was going on around him, but he knew the men had come running to watch, and he could hear them yelling encouragement. A time or two he was able to glimpse

Pete Runyan standing there, hunched over from the pain of his fall, but that pain was a poor second to the one Isaac must be giving him.

The wild pitching gave way to a tired crow-hopping, and gradually that gave way to a hard run, the horse making harsh sounds from deep in its chest, as if it were choking. It had broken into a sweat almost at the beginning, and some of that sweat looked like lather now. But the bay did not give up until exhaustion came. The run slowed to a trot, and the trot to a walk, and finally the bay stopped near Pete Runyan and just stood there trembling, gasping for breath.

Isaac gripped the mane and swung off quickly, stepping out in case the bay might still have strength enough to try to paw him. It did not. Isaac remembered what Pete Runyan had said to him that first day, and now he gave in to a savage temptation to fling it back into the cowboy's face. He handed the rope rein to the surprised Runyan and said, "See there, white boy? All it takes is the knowin' how."

Isaac was swept up in a rush as the cowboys grabbed and shook his hand, pounded him on the back, then pushed and pulled him toward the chuckwagon in jubilation.

Hunter Proffitt was beside himself. "By God, Isaac, you done it. You rubbed his face in it the prettiest ever I seen." Hunter kept shaking Isaac's shoulder so hard that Isaac was afraid he would dislocate it.

Train and one of the other cowboys took charge of the bay to get the saddle off the exhausted animal. Isaac looked back once and saw Pete Runyan standing alone out in that corral, still hunched. Nobody inquired if he was hurt. They were all too busy cheering over his defeat.

Hunter Proffitt broke away and ran ahead to the chuckwagon, to the wide-eyed old cook. "Wash, you got any ruckus juice in that chuckbox that you been savin' for medicine? Ol' Isaac has earned a big snort."

Wash had nothing, or he would have drunk it himself a long time ago. If there was none in the chuckbox, there would be none in camp unless the Major himself kept some stashed. Proffitt caught the Major still off balance, and the Major fetched him a bottle out of his "possibles." Proffitt thumbed the cork out and handled the bottle to Isaac.

Another time he might not have done it, but in his elation—even gloating a little—Isaac took a long drag at the whiskey before passing the bottle back to Proffitt. He lost sight of it after that, but he knew nobody would need to hunt for the cork Proffitt had thrown away.

"Isaac," Proffitt said, slapping him on the back again, "we owe you for this. When we get to town, we're goin' to give you a celebration like you ain't ever seen."

The other cowboys added their agreement, and Isaac enjoyed the glow of his triumph, abetted somewhat by the stiff drink of whiskey he had taken. But directly he glanced at Wash, and he saw disapproval and misgiving in the cook's narrowed eyes.

The first flush gradually died down. Isaac noticed that the men had become quieter. Pete Runyan walked up from the corral, moving slowly, a hand pressed against his bruised and aching ribs. There was still mocking in the faces of the men as they watched him, but they said nothing. Runyan made a point of ignoring them, or at least of trying to.

He paused at the chuckbox, getting a tin cup, then walked to the coffeepot and filled it. He sipped the scalding coffee while every man in camp watched him. Finally he turned, his eyes seeking out Isaac. There was no surrender in them.

"Boy, you couldn't of done it if I hadn't of tired him out for you." He walked through the men, chin high, eyes looking at no one. There was no sign now of a limp, or of hunched shoulders. Whatever the pain, he covered it up.

Isaac knew he had won a point, but he hadn't beaten Pete Runyan.

Chapter Six

They hit Dry Wells in the middle of the afternoon a day ahead of the time the Major had appointed for delivery of the steers to Lon Whitten. The Major rode in to see if Whitten had arrived yet. Isaac was with Joe Sample when the Major came back in an easy trot.

"We got here before he did," he announced. "We'll loose-herd these steers in that draw south of town; the grass is good there."

Joe Sample turned to Isaac with a little of pleasant malice in his eyes. "You know the lay of the land; Pete Runyan don't." He made a sweeping motion with his hand. "You go tell him you're takin' his place on the right point. We'll drift the herd way around and bring it back into that draw from below, where we won't have no steers walkin' into saloons or makin' somebody shinny up a porch post."

Isaac had always called most of the cowboys by their first names, but he had never felt that free toward Pete Runyan. Yet he never wanted to call him *Mister*, either. When Isaac had to call him something, he made it plain *Runyan*. Usually he avoided any name but simply went directly to the matter at hand. "Joe Sample says I'm to take your place on point."

Runyan's resentment was plain. "The hell he did."

"He sure as hell did. You can go argue with him if you want to."

"No argument, boy. You just take the point and see if you can manage to keep this herd out of trouble."

Isaac started, moving his horse in a walk. On signal

from Joe Sample, the cowboys began pushing the cattle, letting them string out into that long, thin line they naturally assumed on the trail. Alf Train was on the left point, opposite. Isaac angled sharply southeastward, giving the town a wide berth, moving only as fast as the steers in front seemed to want to move. Invariably there were certain animals whose nature it was to take the lead and hold it, while the majority were content simply to fall into place and follow. This was a characteristic Isaac had noticed a long time ago about cattle, a characteristic he saw also in men.

There was one red and white spotted steer, lean of leg and long of horn, which Isaac had noticed for several days seemed bent on pushing out in front, hooking belligerently at any others which showed any inclination to crowd him. Though he never said it out loud where anyone could hear him, he had given the steer a name.

"Come on, Pete Runyan," he said quietly as the animal moved out to its place.

The sun was low when Isaac got a signal from Joe Sample to hold his ground. The cowboys let the herd spread out loosely along the draw, where summer rain had freshened the cured grass and had put green back into the crowns. The steers, still sore-footed from the hard pushing of the first couple of days, were content to quit walking and graze awhile.

Presently a buggy topped over a hill in the direction of town, followed by two men on horseback. Isaac saw the Major spur out to meet them. He knew the rig from having seen it so many times before; it belonged to buyer Lon Whitten. And Isaac knew that Whitten always carried a black satchel full of cash beneath the seat of the buggy. Men in this country still retained some distrust toward banks and checks; they liked the honest feel of coin or currency.

He watched the Major tie his horse behind the buggy and climb up into the seat beside Whitten. The two men took their time circling the herd. As they passed Isaac, Whitten called, "You been behavin' yourself, Isaac?"

Isaac grinned and replied, "Yes sir, but only because I don't get no chance to *mis*behave."

He had been seeing Lon Whitten a time or two every year for many years, and he couldn't remember a time Whitten hadn't had a pleasant word for him, and for every other cowboy in the crew. Isaac guessed Whitten knew the difference between white and black, all right, but he never let on that he did, and that counted for something. On Isaac's ledger, Whitten was one of the *good* people, like the Major, and like the Bar L hands.

As the buggy pulled away, Isaac could hear the Major saying something about counting the cattle tomorrow; it was too late in the afternoon to start now.

After supper most of the cowboys began shaving and cleaning up, digging into their warbags for clean but wrinkled clothes, if they had any. The Major called them together and gave each man twenty-five dollars in cash against wages. When he got to Isaac, Isaac shook his head. "I don't need no money, Major. I ain't lost nothin' in that town that I aim to go look for."

Hunter Proffitt stepped up. "Give him the money, Major. He's goin'."

Isaac demurred, but Hunter took the money from the Major's hand and put it firmly into Isaac's. "I told you, Isaac, we owe you a celebration. You're goin' into town with us!"

Isaac didn't want to. The only man in town he counted as a friend was the horse trader, Brady Cunningham, and he knew this crew didn't figure on wasting any time around the wagonyard.

The Major said, "There needs to be a regular guard stood over the herd tonight; how you-all work that out, I'll leave to you. Aside from that you can go to town and raise all the hell you want to, except that I don't want to have to bail anybody out of jail. I don't want any man to take a gun with him, either." He looked at the crew, searching for volunteers. Pete Runyan grunted, "I'll stand the first watch with somebody. I ain't in no hurry for town."

Isaac had rather have stood a double shift of guard than go, but the cowboys swept him along like a chip on a swollen stream, slapping him on the back, telling him what a good time they were fixing to give him for putting Pete Runyan in his proper place.

While the cowboys caught fresh horses from the re-muda, old Wash walked out and beckoned Isaac off with a bony black finger. "Isaac," he warned, his brow deep-wrinkled, "you better watch out for yourself. You're fixin' to get into water a way over your head."

"Just a little celebration, Wash, that's all. I don't relish it, but I don't see as it can hurt none."

"It ain't the celebration so much, it's what that cele-bration is for."

"I don't follow you."

"They all got a peeve on about that Pete Runyan, and they're pattin' you on the back because you outdone him. But sooner or later *some* of them boys, at least, is goin' to remember that, after all, Pete Runyan is a white man. And they're goin' to remember what *you* are."

"These men are my friends."

"You overstep yourself and they won't be."

"You sound like an old woman, Wash."

"But I know my place. I hope to God you know yours."

They loped up the street in a bunch, eight men laughing, shouting, their horses raising a cloud of dust to drift through open doors and windows. No one in Dry Wells would complain so long as they spent their money in liberal amounts. This kind of medicine was what kept the patient alive, even if it sometimes didn't taste too well. Horse trader Cunningham waved at them as they passed his wagonyard, and Isaac had a strong inclination to stop right there. They could talk horses for two hours and never repeat a story. He wondered if Cunningham remembered some of these horses as the same raw broncs he had sold the Major a few weeks ago. The men reined up in front of the Cowboy Bar and Billiard Emporium, squalling and hollering more as if they were finishing a wild evening than just starting one.

Hunter Proffitt shouted, "Come on, Isaac, let's start in on that drinkin' we was talkin' about."

Isaac looked dubiously at the open doors, trying to see into the dim lamplight beyond. "This is old man Digby's place. He told me one time he didn't want me in there."

"The hell with old man Digby. If he wants our

money he'll have to take yours too. There ain't a man on the Bar L outfit that *this* place is too good for." A grin broke across his reddish face. "Unless it'd be Pete Runyan."

The men tied their horses to the hitching posts and stepped up onto the low porch, trying to stomp the dust off their boots, their spurs jingling, their laughter lifting and carrying down the street. They swept into the saloon like a small conquering army, knocking over two or three empty chairs on their surge toward the bar. Hunter Proffitt slapped the flat of his hand upon the mahogany.

"Digby," he declared, "you got whiskey to sell, and we're here to buy. Trot her out."

Digby was a medium-tall man who parted his black hair right down the middle and laid it out flat with some kind of heavy grease; he also favored muttonchop whiskers in full bush. He set a bottle on the bar with his left hand and came up with five glasses clustered on the fingers and thumb of his right. He made a quick count, stopping as he came to Isaac. He fetched two more glasses, one short. "Boys, I'm pleased to have you-all in here, but you know I got a rule." He didn't have to spell it out, but he looked straight at Isaac.

Isaac turned away from the bar, a tightness starting in his stomach. "It's what I was tellin' you, Hunter. You-all have yourselves a time."

Digby said, half apologetic, "It ain't that *I* mind, myself. I don't. But I got some customers that have strong notions. . . ."

Hunter Proffitt leaned over the bar, his smile gone. "Right now, Digby, you got eight customers here, and *we* got some strong notions. Now, ol' Isaac is a Big Lonesome cowpuncher, as good as any and better than most, and if you ever want to sell anything, now or ever again, to *any* Big Lonesome cowpuncher, then you better not turn one of them away."

Digby reconsidered. "Like I say, *I* don't mind. I'd be tickled to sell Isaac a bottle, and he can go set out yonder on the porch and drink it, and nobody in town would say a word."

Proffitt said, "You ain't listenin', Digby. He's goin' to stand right here at this bar and drink with the rest of us, and if you've got somebody that you think is goin' to take *off*ense at it, you just trot him over here to talk to us."

Some of the other cowboys began boisterously backing up Hunter Proffitt's challenge, and Digby motioned worriedly for them to settle down and listen to him. "Now, boys, you know the last thing I ever want in my place is trouble, and I sure ain't goin' to cause you none. If you say you want this boy drinkin' with you, and you're willin' to take the responsibility for him, then it's sure all right with me. I ain't ever been one to deny a man the rights that's due him, not ol' Oscar Digby." He brought one more glass from beneath the mirror that stood on the wall behind the bar, and he set it down in front of Isaac. His mouth smiled, but his eyes did not.

Hunter Proffitt slapped his money on the bar, popped the cork out of the bottle with his thumb, and watched it roll across the floor. One of the cowboys reached down for it, but Proffitt said, "Leave it lay." He filled up the eight glasses and said, "Get one for yourself, Digby." Digby did, and Proffitt filled it for him. "Digby, we're drinkin' to the best black cowboy west of Fort Worth. Here's to the man that beat Pete Runyan." He lifted his glass, and the other cowboys followed his example. So did Digby. Isaac smiled self-consciously and accepted the toast, waiting until the others tipped their glasses up, then he drank his.

Digby wiped the back of his hand across his mouth. "Who is Pete Runyan?"

Proffitt demanded, "You never met Pete Runyan?"

Digby shook his head. "Can't say as I've had the pleasure."

"I'll solemnly vow, Digby, it ain't no pleasure." Proffitt filled the glasses again. "Here's to a man who's lucky enough that he never met Pete Runyan."

It didn't take long for Isaac to begin feeling the warmth of the whiskey in his stomach, and its quick climb to his brain. He had never had any particular fondness for it, and never drank enough of it that he had built up any degree of immunity to its effects. He could begin to sense his vision blurring around the edges. It was as if he were looking at Digby and Proffitt and the others down the length of some sort of tunnel.

Presently the Major came in, and Lon Whitten, carrying his little black bag. They were trailed by six or seven of Whitten's cowboys, and a lanky, mean-eyed man Isaac had always guessed was Whitten's bodyguard, though he did not recall that anyone had ever said so. Carrying so much money around all the time, Whitten probably needed a guard.

After a long, loud session of hand-shaking and greetings, the Major and Whitten retired to a little table in a corner. Whitten set the black bag down by his feet. Isaac noted that all the Whitten cowboys lined up at the bar except the mean-eyed one. He took a chair near Whitten but not at the table. Of all the men in the saloon, he was the only one who took no whiskey. Isaac heard him ask Digby if there was any coffee, and Digby said he would make some.

Most of the Bar L and Whitten cowboys knew each other, by sight if not by name, and a few were good friends from having worked together on other outfits. It didn't take but a bottle or two to make old friends out of all of them, and loud friends.

Isaac lost track of time, the whiskey bringing a rosy glow of well-being over him. He got to thinking maybe this town wasn't so unpleasant, and Oscar Digby wasn't really a bad man after all. Isaac got tired of leaning forward, belly against the bar, and he turned to lean his back against it instead, hooking a bootheel over the rail. He stood that way awhile, watching the Major and Lon Whitten start a game of cards at their table.

A movement at the door caught his eye, and he turned his head. He saw a man standing just out of reach of the lamplight, a vague shadowy figure without a face. Then for a moment the man moved a little closer, looking inside, and he had a face. Isaac blinked in surprise.

He pushed quickly away from the bar. "Hunter, there's Alvin Quain . . . standin' out yonder."

Hunter turned, and so did the other cowboys who had heard. Proffitt stared blankly. "Where?"

"Right there. He was right there in the door a second ago."

Proffitt moved quickly, a little unsteadily, to the door. He stepped out onto the porch, and Isaac followed him.

Proffitt shook his head. "Ain't nobody out here, Isaac."

"But I seen him; I know I did."

Proffitt grinned and took Isaac by the arm, guiding him back into the saloon. "Ain't nobody out there but one gray tomcat. What you seen was the bottom of that glass. Come on, let's fill it up again."

Isaac looked back over his shoulder. "Hunter, I'd swear . . ."

But they poured him another drink, and soon he was doubting it himself. He *had* drunk a right smart.

Presently another face appeared at the door, and this time there was no mistake. Pete Runyan came in. He halted abruptly, seeing the crowd and recognizing them. He turned back as if to leave, then seemed to catch himself. Isaac could read the stubborn thought in the man's face: he was here now, and he would be damned if he would leave for anybody. He moved up to one end of the bar and stood alone. Other men were almost shoulder to shoulder with him, but his manner left no doubt; he was alone, and he intended to stay that way.

Hunter Proffitt had put away a lot of whiskey now, and it was talking loudly. He addressed the whole crowd, but Isaac figured it was meant mostly for Pete Runyan. Proffitt said, "Digby, you told us you hadn't ever met Pete Runyan. Well, that's him over yonder, that feller with his tail between his legs. Ol' Isaac here, he made Pete Runyan stand about two feet tall. You ought to've seen it, Digby, you'd of enjoyed it. Runyan come into camp puffed up like a banty rooster; you never seen a man that thought so much of himself. But Isaac hooked them into him. I tell you, Digby, you'd of busted your sides seein' him set down the way he was. And by a *nigger,* to boot."

Suddenly the whiskey wasn't warm and good to Isaac anymore; it was going sour.

Proffitt had been drinking too long to realize he ought to shut up. "That was the beauty part of it, Digby. It'd of been good if any of us had done it, but for ol'

Isaac to do it, that got him right in the gut. He would sooner of been kicked in the head by a mule."

Proffitt filled Isaac's glass again and shoved it at him. "Here, Isaac, we promised you the damnedest drunk you was ever on, and you ain't but half started yet. Drink up."

Isaac got one glance at Pete Runyan, standing at the bar, looking at nobody. He didn't turn his head that way again. "Hunter, it ain't settin' good on my stomach. I been thinkin' I ought to go back to the herd."

"Go back? Hell no, Isaac, we ain't even started yet."

"I started, and I finished. A little more whiskey and I'll be stretched out on this here floor."

A big idea struck Hunter Proffitt. His face lighted up like a lantern. "What you need, Isaac, is a little exercise. And we know how you can get it. Over at Big Bessie's."

Isaac's mouth dropped open. He was not so drunk that he could not still think. "Not Big Bessie's!"

"Sure, Big Bessie's. Ain't no night in town complete without we all go to Big Bessie's. Ain't that right, boys?" They cheered. A couple of them had their arms around Isaac's shoulders and half pushed, half dragged him to the open door.

Isaac heard Digby call after them, "You-all come back when you're a mind to," though he doubted Digby had any enthusiasm for their return.

Isaac looked desperately to the Major, but the Major was engrossed in his game and was paying no attention.

Isaac fought against the dizziness that made him half helpless, and he wished he never had drunk that whiskey. He could have faked most of it, if he had wanted to. Now, he wondered, why the hell hadn't he? "Hunter, you know I can't go over there. Why, they'd *shoot* me if I was to even stick my head in the door."

"Ain't nobody goin' to shoot you, Isaac. We're all here to protect you." They kept pulling him along despite his protests. Some of the Whitten hands came along too. By the time they got to the front porch where the lantern was hanging, Isaac was almost sober. Cold sweat stood out on his face, and his hands trembled a little.

"Hunter, you got to listen to me. Them's *white* women in there."

"The Big Lonesome is in town tonight," Proffitt declared. "The Big Lonesome boys don't answer to nobody but the Major. You come on, Isaac; you're the guest of honor."

He grabbed at the doorjamb, but they carried him along in a rush. He found himself in the lamp-lit parlor which had bright red-flowered wallpaper and lots of curtains and a big oval rug on the floor. Several couches lined the wall, girls sitting there in gowns of gold and red, showing legs almost up to the knees. Isaac swallowed. He couldn't remember many times he had been more frightened.

A big woman with gold-dyed hair and double chins and huge breasts pushed forward to meet the cowboys. She smiled broadly. "Well, Hunter, you boys come right on in. We been lookin' for you all evenin'." Isaac thought her smile was the brightest he had ever seen, and suddenly he knew the reason. She had a diamond set in one front tooth.

Her smile fell away as she set eyes on Isaac. "Boy, you'll have to go outside and wait. You ought to know better than to come in here."

Proffitt said, "He's with *us*, Bessie."

"I can see that, but he'll have to wait outside. What'll our other company think?"

Proffitt didn't let her faze him. "Bessie, you got no idea what this boy done for us. He's the pride of the Big Lonesome. We brought him in to show him a good time."

"Then go someplace and get him drunk, but take him out of here."

Isaac pulled loose. "She's right, Hunter. I got no business in here."

Proffitt grabbed his arm and dragged him back. "You got as much business in here as anybody. Now, Bessie, ol' Isaac's got money just like the rest of us, and he's willin' to spend it like the rest of us, and you can bank his money just the same as you can bamk ours. We brought him in here to see that he gets a chance to spend a little of it, and you ain't goin' to turn him away."

Bessie said threateningly, "All I got to do is whistle, and . . ."

Proffitt pointed to a piano in the corner. "How much did you pay for that there music box, Bessie?"

"Two hundred dollars, countin' the haul."

"It sure would be a shame if one of these cowboys was to get astraddle of that thing like a bronc and ride it plumb to the ground, wouldn't it?"

Big Bessie paled a little. "Hunter, you wouldn't. . . ."

"Not me, Bessie. I was just sayin' somebody *might*. . . ."

She swallowed, hard. "All right, he can sit here in the parlor and drink whiskey, but that's all he's buyin' in this place."

Proffitt looked up. "Mighty pretty chandelier you got there, Bessie. I was thinkin' how if a feller was ridin' that piano, and he was to rope that chandelier, things could sure look like an awful mess here in the light of mornin'."

Big Bessie trembled in anger, but fear had a strong hold too. "You cowboys are lice, all of you."

"But you sure do like our money," Proffitt said acidly. "Looks like—bad as we hate it—we sort of need each other."

Bessie looked again at Isaac, her eyes hating him. "There ain't no decent white woman . . ."

Proffitt said, "There ain't no decent white woman here."

Bessie turned away to a table where a bottle sat amid a cluster of glasses. She didn't bother to pour into a glass; she just lifted the bottle and drank straight from it. "All right, I got a new girl here, a Mexican girl. She don't know nothin' . . . can't even talk English, hardly. I don't suppose there'd be no great harm." Without looking at the cowboys, she hollered, "María! María, you get yourself out here." She waited a moment and shouted again.

From somewhere down the hall she came, a tiny thing slender as a reed, hair straight and black, tumbling down across her shoulders, framing an olive face that would have been pretty had it not been painted so. Even the painting was amateurishly done; she hadn't been at this long. She stopped at the end of the hall, hesitant about coming out into the parlor.

Impatiently Bessie beckoned her. "Come on out here. *Venga!*"

The girl took three halting steps. She trembled a little.

Hunter Proffitt asked, "Where'd she come from?"

Big Bessie said, "I don't know; Mexico, I guess. Her and some man—husband, I reckon—come through here with an old wagon, headin' God knows where. He took sick and died. She hung around here half-starved. I taken her in. I always been one to take in the poor stranger."

"You sure as hell have, Bessie," Proffitt agreed.

Isaac began backing away. "Hunter, I can't. This thing has gone too far already. I'm goin' back to the wagon."

The cowboys hooted at him. Hunter said, "Anybody that can ride that bay bronc ought not to have no fear for one little ol' Mexican girl. You go on back yonder with her, Isaac. Maybe she'll learn you somethin'. You ain't leavin' here till you've had yourself a time."

They pushed him into the hall. Someone thrust a bottle into his hand. The girl looked back at Bessie, pleading with her eyes, but Bessie motioned her to go on. Head down, she led the way. She opened the door and held it, not looking at Isaac. He hesitated a moment, then shrugged and started through it.

A movement at the end of the hall caught his eye. He had a fleeting glimpse of a man hurrying out the back door.

That, he thought, *is where I ought to be going too.*

The room was small and plain, nothing like the fancy parlor out front. Isaac guessed that by the time they got back this far they weren't looking at the decorations much anyway, most of them. There was the bed and a single chair and a small dresser with a lighted lamp sitting on top of it, alongside a pitcher, a washpan, and a few thin towels.

The girl sat on the edge of the bed, leaving him room. She still hadn't looked at him.

The gown she wore was cut low in front and short

at the bottom, so that her knees showed as she sat on the bed. Isaac looked a moment, and he felt some of the whiskey's warmth coming back to him. Or maybe it wasn't the whiskey. He thought of the bottle in his hand.

"You want a drink?"

She kept looking down. *"No entiendo."*

"A drink. A drink." He held the bottle in front of her face, where she had to look at it. She gave him a brief glance, then shook her head. She was trembling worse now than before.

Scared to death. Coming from Mexico, maybe she ain't never seen nobody as black as me.

He saw a couple of glasses on the dresser, beside the wash basin, and he took one. "Well, *I* am goin' to have *me* a drink." He poured the glass half full and put the bottle on the dresser. He flinched at the burn of the whiskey going down. It was not as good as the stuff over in Digby's saloon, but he would bet Bessie charged twice as much for it. She could get away with it because whiskey was only incidental to her business anyway.

He stared at the girl. "What's your name?"

She glanced at him a little longer this time. *"No entiendo."*

"Your name." He pointed a finger at himself. "Me Isaac. Isaac Jefford. Who are *you?*"

She blinked, not quite comprehending. He remembered then what Bessie had called her. "María, wasn't that your name? María?"

She nodded then, catching his meaning. "María. María Montemayor."

"María's a right pretty name. You're a right pretty girl, or you could be." He glanced at her arm and saw something there, a mark, a bruise perhaps. He reached out to touch it and she quickly drew away, fear rising quickly in her face. He pulled his hand back. "Sorry, María, I didn't go to scare you none. I been scared enough tonight for both of us. I'm still a little scared, just bein' in here."

His voice was quiet and gentle, and it seemed to reassure her a little. But he made up his mind he wasn't going to make any sudden move with his hand again. He sat back in the chair, studying her face. She dropped her gaze under his intent scrutiny, but then she lifted her eyes again, curiosity gradually taking the place of fear.

Isaac got up from the chair and poured some water out of the pitcher into the basin. He dipped one of the towels in it and wrung it out. He touched the towel to the surprised girl's face. "Hold still," he said quietly, "I just want to get some of this damned ugly paint off." She recovered quickly from the surprise and held steady while he wiped off the powder and rouge. Done, he put his fingers under her chin and turned her head toward the lamp so he could get a better look at her face, without the shadows.

"See there, that's a whole lot prettier now. You got a right nice-lookin' face when it's cleaned up to where a man can see it."

She said something in Spanish that he did not understand. He had never been around Mexican people much. He shook his head. "I'm sorry, little girl. I don't understand a word you're sayin'."

He sat down in the chair again, staring at her. She seemed to have lost most of her fear now. "Seems to me like you're too young to be in a place like this, and too pretty. But I guess life don't always ask us what we'd like to have. If it did, I reckon I'd of asked for a lighter-complected skin than the one I got."

It struck him odd; this thought had crossed his mind many times in the past, but this was the first time he had ever put it into words. He supposed he wouldn't have said it this time either, had he not known the girl couldn't understand any of it. He gave the matter a second thought. "Now, that's a damnfool thing to say. There ain't nothin' wrong with this skin; if the good Lord hadn't of had some good reason to want me to have it, He wouldn't of give it to me. I beat ol' Pete Runyan, didn't I? Him with his white skin and all, but I beat him just the same. I got no call to apologize for this hide of mine."

She kept looking at him, the fear gone, a little of amusement beginning to show in her dark eyes.

He said, "You think it's funny, don't you, me runnin' on and on thisaway and you not understandin' a thing I say?"

She said something in Spanish. He nodded, though he had not the slightest idea what she was talking about. Encouraged, she talked on, voice getting faster and faster, her hands lifting and gliding and dancing as she talked. He would nod and smile, carried away by the spell of her, and by the glow of the whiskey in his blood. He sat back, fascinated, until finally she had talked herself out.

He knew it had been a long time since she had talked so much, in a sense imprisoned in an alien place, hearing only an alien tongue. He said, "I'm sorry we can't understand each other . . . or maybe we *do* understand each other. Not the words, but the rest of it. We're some ways alike, me and you. We're both misfits here, caught in a place that's not noways ours but with noplace else to go."

He saw the beauty in her eyes, and he wanted simply to keep looking and keep smiling. But a cold thought settled upon him like a heavy gray cloud. That beauty would not remain in her eyes long, not if she stayed here. And she *would* stay here; she had no way to get out. "Girl . . . pretty girl . . . you're like a bird somebody's caught and put in a cage. It'd of been better if they'd just shot and killed you. This way, you're already dead, only you're still walkin' around. That's the hell of it . . . you got to keep on walkin' around."

His big fists clenched in helplessness. He studied the floor, thinking, but knew there was not a thing in this world he could do to help her. Gently he said, "Girl, there's been times I got to feelin' sorry for myself. But if I ever do it again, I hope the good Lord smites me hip and thigh. At least they ain't caught me in no cage." He stood up, his face grave. "I never did have no use for a damned town. After this, I don't think I ever *will* have."

She saw he was about to leave, and she was puzzled. She asked a question and motioned toward the bed. He shook his head.

"It ain't that I wasn't sorely tempted, at first. Now it'd be like spillin' whiskey in church." Reaching into his pocket, he pulled out what he still had left of the money the Major had given him; he hadn't spent but a few dollars of it. He put it into her hand and closed her fingers over it. She stared at him, not understanding.

"Don't you worry none about it, little girl; you've given me more than my money's worth. I wisht there was some way I could help you get out of here, but all I can do is give you this money. The rest I'll have to leave up to the good Lord. You may talk to Him different, but I expect your God is the same one that always looked after me."

He looked up the hall to be sure none of the cowboys was watching. He could hear laughter up in the parlor. He waved to the girl and quietly closed the door behind him. For all Big Bessie needed to know, he was there for the night; maybe she would leave the girl alone.

He tiptoed a dozen steps to the back door, opened it quickly, and stepped out into the darkness. All he wanted now was to walk back to where his horse was tied and get to camp. He dodged the patches of lamplight because some of the Bar L cowboys might happen to see him. He moved up the street past the livery barn, toward the mercantile.

That was when he heard the shots.

Chapter Seven

Isaac paused in midstride, startled. His first thought was that someone was celebrating a mite loud. But he heard somebody yell, and then the boom of a shotgun, fired twice. The whiskey's warmth was gone; he felt suddenly cold and afraid.

The shooting came from the saloon. He thought, *The Major! Somebody's killin' the Major!* He started running hard. He saw three men spill out through the lamplight that marked the saloon door and run to horses tied outside. The animals reared and plunged in fright at the shooting and the sudden rush of the men. One horse broke its reins and came galloping down the street, pitching a little. Isaac heard someone shout, "Just grab you one, Quain."

Quain! *Then I was right; I did see him.*

The men swung into the saddles and spurred down the street toward him. Isaac stepped over quickly to get out of their way and found himself in a dim patch of lanternlight shining off the porch of Handley's mercantile. He saw old man Handley standing up there on the wagon dock, staring in wonder.

Isaac was aware that one horseman was coming straight at him. A harsh voice shouted, "Isaac!"

He could see only the shadowy outline, but he knew the man. He saw a flash and felt the sting of splinters as a bullet smacked into the loading dock near him. Handley raced for the door with a speed that belied his age. Heart bobbing, Isaac dived under the loading dock.

He heard a rider shout, "What the hell, Quain?"

Quain replied, "I got me a nigger to kill!" He rode

his horse up close to the dock. Isaac caught a short
breath and scrambled farther, trying to reach the low
opening that went under the floor of the mercantile. It
was pitch black under there.

The rider warned, "Kill one some other time. We got
to get out of here."

Quain snarled. "Isaac!" and sent two more shots
under the dock. But he could not see his quarry, and the
shots were wild. Isaac heard him curse, then spur away
to catch up with the other two riders who were going off
and leaving him.

Isaac stayed a minute on hands and knees, nausea
rushing over him, the whiskey trying to come up. He
started crawling, not straightening up until he was out
from under the dock. Then he flattened again, for men
stood on the porch of the saloon, firing blindly through
the dust and the darkness in the direction the riders had
gone. Isaac was just at the edge of the line of fire. He lay
there, his head down, until the firing stopped. He saw
men running for horses, spurring out in ragged disorder.
Isaac pushed to his feet, trembling a little. Kelly Haskell,
Lon Whitten's foreman, was leading the pursuit.

They'll never catch them, Isaac thought, *not
thataway.*

Staying close to the building to avoid being run over
by the horses, he trotted to the saloon and jumped up
onto the porch. He stopped at the door, dreading to go
in.

It ain't goin' to get no better for puttin' it off.

He had to step over a man who lay in the open
doorway, face on the floor. There was no question about
it, this man was dead.

To his immediate relief he saw the Major kneeling in
the corner by a fallen man. At first glance he sensed that
the Major was unhurt. But there had been violence
enough here. Tables and chairs were turned over. The
room was clouded by gunsmoke so heavy that it pinched
his nose and set his eyes to burning. The barkeeper Digby
and Pete Runyan were bent over a man who lay on the
floor near the bar, groaning. This was the man Isaac had
always figured to be Lon Whitten's bodyguard.

Isaac moved up to the Major, and through the

smoke he saw that the man stretched out in the corner was Lon Whitten. Isaac's tongue moved across dry lips as he stared in shock. The Major glanced up, and Isaac said, "Major . . ."

The Major nodded grimly. "Yes, Isaac, he's dead."

Isaac didn't even look for Lon Whitten's black bag; he knew it was gone. "They come to rob Mister Whitten?"

"It happened fast. Nobody had a chance to do anything."

"Alvin Quain was with them."

"I saw him. My guess is that Quain was at the foot of this. He was with us long enough to know how we operate. He knew we would be meeting Lon here with the cattle; he knew Lon would be bringing a lot of cash with him, like he always did. Somewhere he fell in with evil companions and they hatched this scheme." The Major studied Isaac a moment. "It's a good thing he didn't see you, Isaac."

"He did see me, Major. I was comin' up the street. He took some shots at me."

The Major's voice sharpened, and he saw the blood from the splinters. "You're hit. . . ."

"No sir, it was dark out there, and I skedaddled under the loadin' dock at Handley's, and then under the buildin'. Quain didn't hardly have time to crawl in under there and get me."

The Major swore bitterly. "If I'd only brought a gun."

Isaac saw a pistol lying by Lon Whitten's body. "Looks like Mister Whitten's didn't do him no good. A gun would've got you killed, Major."

A crowd was pushing noisily into the saloon, demanding to know what had happened. Digby began telling with much excitement, repeating himself frequently, how four men had come in singly over a period of several minutes as if strangers to each other, looking only for a drink, and how, at some signal which he hadn't seen or heard, they suddenly threw down on everybody in the room. Whitten's bodyguard had resisted and had been severely wounded. Whitten had drawn a pistol to defend himself and had been shot through the heart.

Someone pulled the dead man in out of the doorway and turned him over, holding a lamp down close to his face. "Who is this?" a voice demanded.

"One of the robbers," Digby said, voice still quavering. "In all the excitement, Pete Runyan here jumped behind the bar and come up with my double-barreled shotgun. This one had Lon Whitten's black bag. Runyan gave him both barrels. But one of the others grabbed the bag and got off with it."

A chilling thought came to Isaac for the first time. "If they got the money, Major, how you goin' to get paid for the herd?"

The Major shook his head, blinking. "It hadn't crossed my mind."

"Looks to me like you lost a buyer, Major."

The Major looked down at his friend. "This is no time to be concerned about a thing like that." But he pondered a minute and added, "But it *is* time, I guess. It comes to me, Isaac, that I'm in bad trouble."

The Bar L cowboys came hurrying up from Big Bessie's, brought in a run by a mistaken report that the Major had been shot. Hunter Proffitt sighed in relief. "I'm glad it was him instead of you, Major."

The Major gave him a sharp look of reproach, and Proffitt retracted a little. "I mean, if it had to be one of you. I'm sorry it was anybody."

The Major said, "Joe Sample stayed at the wagon, didn't he?"

Proffitt nodded. "He stayed so more of us could go."

The Major looked up at Alf Train. "I wish you'd fetch Joe here; I'm likely to need him."

Isaac offered to go, but the Major said Quain had tried to shoot him once tonight, and he didn't want Isaac out there in the dark.

About the time Joe Sample rode up to the saloon, Kelly Haskell and the others who had chased after the robbers came straggling back, slumped in discouragement. Haskell stood in the door, face bitter as he looked across the room at Lon Whitten's body. It still lay where it had been, blanket-covered to await the arrival of the law. "Too dark out there. They got away from us. But we'll be up and trackin' at first light." He moved reluctantly across the room and stood over his employer, slowly taking off his hat and crushing it in his hands. "I reckon I knew he was dead as soon as he hit the floor, but I kept hopin'. . . ." He looked around for the wounded bodyguard. "Where's Johnson?"

"They took him down the street," the Major replied. "The doctor is working on him."

"Odd thing," Haskell said. "Ol' Lon paid Johnson's wages for two years just to stay close and keep him out of trouble. First time anybody makes a try to take Lon's money . . ."

"It was too fast, and there were too many of them."

"I ain't blamin' Johnson especially. I'm blamin' myself too. I was sittin' over yonder with a whiskey in my hand. If I'd of had my wits about me, maybe *I* could of done somethin'. Only man in the place that made a move was that man of yours." He motioned toward Pete Runyan.

Runyan looked at him but said nothing. Kelly Haskell thrust out his big rough hand. "Friend, I'd like to shake with you."

Pete Runyan accepted the handshake. "I didn't save your boss."

"But you made them pay a price for him. The one you shot won't ever kill anybody else. I just wisht you could've shot them all."

Isaac saw something happening among the Bar L cowboys. They were sobering fast, and it was soaking in on them that Pete Runyan was the only man to draw blood against the robbers. Hunter Proffitt looked at the double-barreled shotgun lying on the bar. "That the one you done it with, Runyan?"

Runyan didn't answer him. Proffitt walked to the bar and picked up the shotgun, breaking it open, catching one of the two expended cases that fell out of it. Some of the cowboys followed after Proffitt, and they passed the shotgun around among themselves.

Barkeeper Digby said, "That's the one, all right. It's mine. Naturally I'd of used it myself, but I was standin' over yonder in the corner when everything commenced. Wasn't no way I could get back. You ought to've seen

Runyan, though. Quickest thing ever I seen, the way he jumped across that bar and come up with that gun."

Hunter Proffitt's eyes showed a change. There was a beginning of admiration in them instead of the old disdain. "You done good, Runyan."

Runyan only nodded and turned his back. He poured himself a drink from a bottle on the bar and stood there, in the midst of the crowd but somehow nevertheless alone.

The Major motioned for Kelly Haskell to sit down, and Haskell took a chair beside him. The Major passed him a bottle, and Haskell tilted it to his lips, not waiting or looking for a glass.

The Major said, "This may not seem the time to talk about such a thing, Kelly, but I'm afraid this has put me in a bad situation. I had those cattle sold to Lon Whitten."

"Major, whatever agreement was between you and Lon, I'm afraid it's blown to hell. With him dead and the money gone, there's nobody left to honor the deal, and no money to pay for it. You've still got your cattle. You're free now to sell them to somebody else."

"But who, Kelly?"

"Drive them up to Dodge City and sell them at the railroad; that's what Lon was goin' to do. He figured he could take a profit on them over and above the price he was payin' you. Drive them up there and take the profit for yourself."

"But I haven't the time. That's why I was selling them to Lon here, so I could have the cash. I've got less than two weeks to deliver payment into the hands of J. Warren Norris in Fort Worth. Otherwise he'll foreclose and take me over."

Kelly Haskell eyed the Major speculatively. Evidently he knew nothing about the Major's financial condition. "You've got a steer herd here that ought to be good collateral. Get the man to give you an extension till you can get the cattle up to the railroad. Give him a little bonus on the interest."

"J. Warren Norris doesn't want interest; he doesn't want to see the loan paid at all. He wants to take me over. Under no circumstances would he lift a finger to help me out of this trouble."

Haskell frowned darkly. "One of *them* kind of thieves? Ol' Lon, he always hated that kind of a robber worse than one that used a gun. I wisht I knew somethin' that would help you, Major." He took a shot of the whiskey, and his face lighted a little. "Maybe I *do*. You know ol' Shanghai Pierce?"

"Everybody knows Shanghai Pierce," the Major said.

"Ol' Shang has started up from the lower country with two herds, bound for the railroad. If you could catch him somewheres with these cattle, and offer them to him at a price where he could make money, I'll bet he'd buy them off of you, cash in hand on delivery."

"He wouldn't be likely to have that kind of money with him. And I've got to have cash."

"Shanghai Pierce can walk into any bank in the state of Texas and draw a draft for any amount he wants, just on his face."

The Major considered the idea, and it was evident he saw merit in it. "But finding him in time and getting these cattle to him . . ."

Haskell looked around for the barkeeper. "Digby, you got a piece of paper back there someplace, and a pencil?"

When Digby brought them, Haskell started sketching a rough map. "The reason I know all this, Lon was figurin' how to beat ol' Shang to the railroad with this set of cattle he was buyin' off of you. He figured the market might be a little better before Shang got there than it would be after he muddies the waters. Now, accordin' to Lon's information, Shang's got two herds on the trail, a day apart. He left the Nueces on the fourteenth. Me and Lon, we sat down and figured out how he was goin' to route them cattle, and how many miles a day they was apt to travel. We figured to work northeast from here, push these steers of yours pretty hard the first two–three days, hit the main trail up yonder, and cut in ahead of Shang by a full day, or maybe even two days . . . the more the better."

Major Lytton frowned over the map. "Now, what if

we drove straight east instead of northeast, and cut into the trail at the nearest point?"

"It'd take some close figurin'. Allowin' nine miles a day . . ." Haskell's voice trailed off into a mumble as he started calculating, estimating distances, adding up days and miles. "I'd say the chances are big you'd come in too late, and you'd cut in behind him. Best thing is to angle northward a little and intercept him higher up on the trail, but not as high as me and Lon figured to go."

The Major took the map, sketching in streams and landmarks. He motioned Joe Sample over, although Sample had been close enough to watch from the beginning. "That's the Clear Fork, and that's the Salt Fork. Now, we're here, and nearest I can figure, that point on the trail is about a hundred miles. At nine miles a day, that's eleven days."

"Eleven days might be too late, Major. To be safe you better make it in eight or nine. Ol' Shang is a cattle-drivin' son-of-a-gun." Joe shook his head. "It'll take some doin', pushin' those cattle that far in eight days, or even nine."

The Major looked at him. "Did you ever work for J. Warren Norris?"

"No sir, never did."

"If we don't make that trip in eight or nine days, you *will* be working for J. Warren Norris."

At the bar, Hunter Proffitt and two or three of the Bar L cowboys were still watching Pete Runyan. At length Proffitt made the overture. "Runyan, I'd be tickled to buy you a drink."

Pete Runyan didn't look at him. "I thought you done all your buyin' for your *black* friend."

"No hard feelin's meant."

Runyan turned, his eyes narrowed and angry. "No? Then how come you kept throwin' that boy in my face the way you done?"

"You just got our goat for a little while, is all. We'd be glad to forget that, after what you done here."

Pete Runyan's eyes found Isaac, and Isaac thought he saw some dark humor in them. "At least I wasn't hidin' under a loadin' dock."

Stung, Isaac said, "I didn't have no gun. What else could I do?"

"If you'd of had a gun, you'd of probably still been hidin' under that loadin' dock. I never seen a black boy yet that wouldn't show the white feather."

Anger boiled in Isaac, anger and a sense of unjust accusation. "There wasn't nothin' I could do."

Ordinarily Isaac would have backed away from the argument then and there, but the anger was too strong. "There was somethin' *you* could've done. You could've saved one barrel of that gun and kept them from gettin' off with the money. But you got rattled and fired both barrels into one man."

Runyan stepped away from the bar, raising his fist. "Boy . . ."

The Major snapped impatiently, "Stop it, both of you. Have a little respect for a good man lying here dead."

Chapter Eight

Next morning they had their horses caught and saddled as soon as it was light enough to tell a white horse from a black one. They had Wash's chuckwagon loaded with enough supplies for the trip so they did not have to put up with the encumbrance of the hoodlum wagon. As the cowboys prepared to line out and get the steers up from the bedground, Kelly Haskell rode in at the head of the Whitten crew. The Major gravely shook Haskell's hand and offered the men breakfast.

Haskell shook his head. "We had ours, Major, thanks."

"I'd be tickled to hire you-all to help us push this herd. We could use all the help we can get."

Haskell looked around at his men. "That's a temptin' offer, Major, seein' as we're all of a sudden out of work. But I reckon we owe it to Lon Whitten to try to make those fellers pay for what they done. It'll soon be light enough that we can start cuttin' for sign."

The Major nodded in sympathy for their feelings. "You men be careful. If you catch up with them, remember that they've already killed. No reason to think they won't do it again."

Grimly Haskell said, "We intend to kill them first. If we catch them, the law won't be out no expense for a trial—just for an inquest. Good luck to you on your drive." Haskell extended his hand, then he touched spurs to his horse and rode away in a trot, his men closely following him.

The Major watched them a minute or two, gritting

his teeth hard. Finally he turned back to Joe Sample and Proffitt and Isaac and the others. "It's up to you-all now. You know where this herd needs to intersect the trail, and you know how little time you've got to get there in. I'll ride straight east and find Shanghai Pierce so we can get the deal settled and he can have the cash in hand by the time his herds reach you."

He turned to Wash, and Wash handed him a sackful of food. He tied this behind the cantle with the two blankets he had rolled there. He swung up onto his horse, then looked down, his gaze falling upon first Isaac, then Hunter Proffitt, then finally Pete Runyan. "I know there's been disagreement between some in this camp, even animosity. But I'm counting on all of you to put that aside. The only thing which matters now is to get this herd there on time. As for anything else, if you can't forget it, at least defer it." He raised his hand in farewell. "Get them moving, Joe."

Joe Sample nodded. "We'll be there waitin' for you, Major."

The Major rode east, into the rosy smear of color spreading across the horizon.

Isaac watched him until he was jarred by the harsh voice of Pete Runyan. "All right, pet, he's gone. Now get yourself set to do a man's work or get the hell out of the way."

Isaac turned on him. "I'll out-do anything *you* can do, Runyan." Not Pete, not *Mister* Runyan, just *Runyan*. It was not a big thing, on the surface, but it was a way of claiming equality, if not even superiority. It did not pass unnoticed.

Runyan said, "I'm *sir* to you, boy."

"When hell is froze over with ice six foot thick."

Isaac heard a sound from Wash, a sort of a whimper. He saw dismay in the old cook's face, and pleading in the dark eyes. He caught the censure in Joe Sample's voice. "All right, let's get that herd up and movin'. Isaac, you take the left point. That'll keep you out of harm's way."

Pete Runyan looked surprised and a little scandalized. The point was a position of responsibility and even of honor. Runyan said, "And, Isaac, you better move along at a right smart clip, else I'll see that them cattle run over you. There won't be no loadin' dock out yonder to crawl under."

"I'll set you a pace," Isaac said sharply. "Let's see if you can keep up with it."

Isaac moved out a little way from the herd, getting his bearings. One-eyed Alf Train was opposite him on the right, a quiet steady man as dependable as a lead ox. There was no compass; a man went by the feeling in his bones. On long trail drives across unaccustomed country, wagon cooks would often line their wagontongues on the north star at night so they would know their direction the next morning. Isaac didn't think he needed that. Growing up in this prairie country had given him a keen sense of direction. Once in a while a long spell of cloudy weather threw him off, but right now he had the sun to go by.

The cowboys brought up that red and white spotted steer which always wanted to assume the lead. The other steers instinctively followed. Even in bovine society there was that natural tendency toward leadership on the part of a few, and that tendency simply to follow on the part of the many. The big steer had had a few challengers as the herd was being moved down to Dry Wells, but he had put them in their place. Now none sought to contest his right to lead, though as the long walk began they hooked and jabbed and ran at each other in their contest for the trailing positions. These were gradually settled one by one, and each steer of a contentious nature found his place in the pecking order.

Isaac looked at the spotted steer with a mixture of admiration and malice. "I swear, ol' boy, you're just like that Pete Runyan; you think you stand above the whole world. But one of these days you'll run onto another critter that don't take none of that, and he'll just naturally clean your plow. I hope by God he's a black one!"

Isaac set a pace that would put the steers into the fastest walk they could maintain without breaking into a trot. Behind him, the cowboys pushed the cattle just enough to maintain that pace. Though cattle could be trotted or even run for a short distance, to try it on a long drive would be ruinous.

Being steers they were mostly quiet, a few bawling

for traveling partners they had lost. Every so often Isaac enjoyed turning in the saddle, especially when he was working up a gentle rise and could look back upon the herd a little below him. It was a sight that never failed to please him, those cattle strung out most of a mile in single and double and triple file, a dozen or so horsemen spotted at intervals on either flank, Wash's tarp-covered wagon off two hundred yards or so on the upwind side to be free of dust. However, the dust was not bad here, for the grass was thick and green; summer rains had been favorable. The earth was carpeted so that the hoofs did not cut through to scar the ground and loosen the earth as they would in a drier time.

Except for these cattle and these cowboys, there was nothing anywhere in sight to show that man had been here or made his mark. To Isaac's way of thinking, this was good. He often wished he could have been here to see this country before any other man had ever come, or at least to have seen it as the Indians saw it. Most of man's marks were a disturbance of God's work rather than an enhancement, he believed. He was pessimist enough to expect that man would eventually ruin this.

He watched a sleek band of antelope grazing in the distance, their white tails like puffs of cotton. They jerked their heads up at sight of him and of the cattle which followed him. They broke into a run, taking a long circle in single file, passing in front of him, pausing on a distant rise for a curious look back, then moving on over and out of sight.

Every so often he spooked a long-legged jackrabbit, which would skitter away in a zigzag pattern through the grass, pause like the antelope to look back and reappraise the danger, then continue its flight if it was pressed. The smaller cottontail could not run so fast or so far but usually had a hole somewhere nearby into which it would disappear, its hind legs throwing up a thin shower of dirt as it scurried down to safety.

Isaac smiled. He knew men who would shoot these rabbits as sport, or try to, but he had never killed them except for meat, and that only in hardship. He always figured if God had not wanted them here He would not have put them where He did.

Now and again he spotted loose cattle in the line of the drive, usually cows and calves, heifers or steers considered too young to go to market. He would trot out ahead of the herd and chase them off to keep them from becoming mixed up in the trail cattle. It took less time to keep them out than to have to go in later and cut them out.

Sometime about midmorning he heard the rattle of trace chains and turned to see Wash pushing his team in a trot, moving out ahead of the herd so he could set up and have dinner ready by the time the cowboys reached him. Isaac waved as the cook went by him, but all he got back from Wash was a critical look he did not understand.

The sun was about straight up when he spied Wash's wagon ahead of him, the smoke curling from the cook-fire. Wash had camped partway up the side of a hill, probably reasoning that the herd could pass beneath and downwind of him. Cowboys did not relish dust settling on their biscuits and floating on their coffee. Isaac waved as he passed a hundred yards below Wash, but Wash gave no evidence he was looking. Isaac's stomach rumbled a little. However, he rode on, turning to watch half the cowboys peel away from the herd and lope to the chuckwagon.

He had made the better part of another mile before he heard a horse coming up behind him. Chalk Denson said, "Joe Sample sent me to hold down your place while you eat, Isaac."

Isaac nodded. "Thanks, Chalk. Dusty back there?"

"Not bad. But you got it awful easy up here, ain't you?"

Isaac had an uneasy feeling the cowboy's smile was forced. "It's all right," Isaac said. "A little lonesome."

He stopped short of the wagon and tied his horse to a bush. The first cowboys to eat had gone back to the herd, and the second half of the crew was here now. They were too busy with their plates to have much to say. Isaac went to the chuckbox for his plate and cup and utensils, then out to the pots and Dutch ovens. Plate full, he made his way to his usual eating place on the wagontongue. He dug in hungrily. There never was much variety about old Wash's cooking, but when a man was hungry enough variety didn't mean much. Isaac was aware that Pete Runyan was squatted against a wagon wheel and occasionally casting a glance his way, but Isaac turned a little more to the side where he didn't have to see him. Losing the hoodlum wagon had cost Runyan his accustomed place.

As Isaac finished his plate, Joe Sample dumped his own plate into the washtub, then moved up to stand by the wagontongue. "Isaac," he frowned, "you see anything out there this mornin'?"

Isaac glanced at him, puzzled. "Nothin' unordinary. Why?"

"I wasn't thinkin' too much when I put you on the point. It's got to worryin' me that we don't know whichaway Alvin Quain and them others went last night. I got to thinkin' we might ride up on them unexpectedly, and there you'd be—way out front, by yourself."

Isaac had had the same thought a time or two this morning but had dismissed it. "Them fellers is on the dodge. I doubt they'll let a whole trail herd of cattle slip up on them unawares."

"Just the same, you're exposed out there. If you want me to, I'll move you back on the herd somewhere."

Pete Runyan spoke up. "I'll be glad to take your place, Isaac, if you're scared."

Even if Isaac had been tempted to relinquish the position, he would not now. "I'll be all right."

Runyan said, "Maybe Joe *wants* you to give up the point, and he's just tryin' to save your feelin's by not sayin' so." Isaac looked at Runyan, not quite comprehending. Runyan added, "Maybe it just don't look right, Isaac, you bein' up in front of everybody. You belong in the rear, not in the front."

Joe Sample took that as a challenge to his authority. Even if he had been thinking of replacing Isaac on the point, he could not afford to do so now. "Runyan," he said tightly, "I'm the one in charge here, not you. I say who rides point and who rides drag. I'm sorely tempted to put you on the drags." But Sample wouldn't do that, either, not after what Pete Runyan had done last night. "If you-all have finished eatin', we got places to go."

Sample unstrapped the carbine and its scabbard

from his own saddle. "Isaac, I'd feel better if you took my saddlegun." Isaac accepted the offer with thanks. The only weapon he owned was an old pistol, and he always left that in his warbag, rolled up with his bedding. There wasn't much call for a pistol these days.

Isaac changed horses and loped up to take his position, letting Chalk Denson come back to a place on the left swing. Isaac knew the waterhole which Joe Sample wanted to make for the night, and he knew it would take a steady pace all afternoon and probably to dark. He would pick out a point on the horizon and ride straight toward it, then pick out another point beyond and make for that, or just a little to the right or left of it, as his sense of direction dictated. Once in a while when he thought the spotted steer was slowing up, Isaac would move in and push him a little.

The afternoon passed without event. It seemed to him they never would make that waterhole, and a vague suspicion gnawed at him that he might have let himself stray off course. Wash moved his chuckwagon on ahead of the herd late in the afternoon, somewhat later than Isaac thought he should. He decided Wash had thought over what Joe had said about those robbers. The last thing in this world Wash would have wanted to do would be to ride up on them by himself.

But just as dusk closed in, Isaac saw the trees, and up the slope a quarter mile from the waterhole was the flicker of firelight where Wash had stopped the wagon, far enough from the hole to let the herd water without crowding the camp. Isaac had to take only a slight swing to the right, Alf Train dropping away on his own point to compensate, to lead the herd straight into the appointed place.

Joe Sample came loping up. "Good job, Isaac. The Major always did say you had the best sense of direction he ever saw in anybody but an Indian. You sure you ain't got a little Indian blood in there someplace?"

Isaac smiled a little wearily. "The folks that owned my people, they wasn't partial none to Indians." He let the smile go, for it was an effort to arouse it anyway. "You want me to ride drag tomorrow, Mister Joe?"

Sample looked surprised. "What makes you think that?"

"You got yourself in a little of a bind, puttin' me on point. I won't mind if you take me off of it."

"That would make it look like Pete Runyan had won a hand."

Isaac shrugged, not liking the idea but resigned to it. "I take my pleasure in small packages. You left me up here all day."

Joe Sample studied the proposition soberly. "We'll see."

The steers had had no water all day, so they began breaking into a trot. Isaac and Alf Train and Joe Sample loped up to stay even with the leaders, cutting ahead finally to water their horses before the steers stirred the mud. The horse wrangler had already brought the remuda forward and had watered it before the cattle. And even ahead of the wrangler, Wash had watered his team and filled his barrels.

The cowboys held back and gave the cattle plenty of room while they drank their fill of water. Many would drift away, then come back for a second drink. It was the better part of an hour before Joe Sample was satisfied and signaled for the men to move the cattle off to bedground. The grass was short here, the ground bare in large patches because of heavy grazing in close proximity to the water. Before the cattle had come, the buffalo had probably given this place hard use. Huge buffalo wallows were still in evidence, their edges grown up in rank weeds from the water which collected there when it rained.

The first nightguard shift went to the wagon to eat while the other men got the cattle bedded down. When they came back to assume the bobtail watch over the herd, the rest of the crew went to the wagon, unsaddled, and trooped up to the chuckbox. As was his custom, Isaac bided his time until everyone else had served himself.

Wash came over and sat down near him on the wagontongue and began to complain about the difficulty of cooking like this. He was used to making camp on roundups, where he had a day or two—at least—in every place he dropped the wagontongue. "The beans are tough," Wash said resentfully. "How am I supposed to cook beans when they don't give me time?"

"Cook them at night," Isaac suggested. "Then all you got to do is warm them up the next day."

"It ain't no fit way for a man to have to cook." Wash was careful not to talk loudly enough for anybody besides Isaac to hear. "They're blamin' me because the beans ain't done, but it ain't noway my fault."

"I ain't heard nobody complain."

"They *are*, though, just the way they're lookin'. They don't have to say it out loud. And you sure ain't helpin' things none, rilin' them the way you been doin'."

"What have I done?"

"Ridin' point way off up there by yourself, sittin' up in the saddle proud as if you was white. It don't set well with them, Isaac."

"I ain't heard nobody complain about that either, nobody but Runyan."

"You ain't *wantin'* to hear, is all. They won't say nothin' direct to you because they figure you're the Major's pet. But they'll sure take it out on *me*, and no mistake."

"You're lettin' your imagination run away with you."

"Think it's imagination, do you? You just wait, Isaac Jefford. You just wait and see." Wash stomped off to his chuckbox, stepping well around Pete Runyan. Isaac watched him narrowly, not wanting to put stock in Wash's fears. He had always been as scary as an old hen.

On the other side of the cookfire a cowboy coughed. Pete Runyan said, "What's the matter, Curly? Dust get you?"

The cowboy nodded. "It got a little bad this afternoon, ridin' back with the drags."

Runyan glanced in Isaac's direction. "I ain't heard Isaac cough. Must be pretty nice up where *he's* been."

Isaac tensed. He realized Runyan was baiting him, and he decided to ignore it. *Only time a fish ever gets caught is when he opens his mouth and grabs the hook,* he thought. He avoided looking at Runyan.

Runyan's next comment was made directly at Isaac.

"I said, Isaac, I don't expect it was very dusty up on the point, was it?"

Isaac found he was spilling some of his coffee, and he caught himself. He still did not look at Runyan or attempt to answer him.

Pete Runyan pushed to his feet, dropped his plate and cup in the tub, then moved a couple of steps closer to Isaac, "Maybe it *was* dusty up there after all; seems like dust must've got in his ears." He took another step. "Look at me, Isaac, when I'm talkin' to you."

Isaac could not ignore that. He looked, his eyes hardening in growing anger. He did not trust himself to say anything.

Runyan demanded, "How about it, Isaac? You goin' to let Curly have your place tomorrow and you ride back with the drags where you belong?"

Isaac pushed up from the wagontongue, his fist knotting.

Joe Sample stepped in front of him, his voice brittle. "I told you once today, Pete. If you're worried about Curly, I can let him have your place and you can ride the drag tomorrow. I put Isaac up there on *my* judgment, not on his, and he stays up there till I get ready to put him somewhere else. Now, if you got any further objections to the way I run this outfit, it's a wide-open country in every direction, and I'm sure there's parts of it that you've never seen."

Pete Runyan tried to stare Joe Sample down. If it had come to a contest, Runyan probably could have beaten Sample by virtue of his greater weight and a considerably smaller burden of years. But Sample would have been fighting all the way down. Pete Runyan backed off.

"I didn't mean no challenge to you, Joe. It just puts the gravel in my craw when I see *him* actin' uppity."

"Isaac ain't uppity. When the Major's here, he does what the Major tells him, and he don't never talk back. When the Major's not here, he does what *I* tell him. You better decide to do the same or go hunt you another place to work."

Runyan appeared on the verge of doing just that. But he didn't. "It was the Major that I hired to, and when I leave this outfit it'll be the Major that I quit to." He walked away from Joe Sample, out by himself to where the saddles had been dropped when the horses were turned loose, where the wrangler would shortly bring the remuda for the men to catch their night horses.

Joe Sample moved slowly out in the opposite direction. When he was fifty yards from the wagon he looked back at Isaac and beckoned with a curt jerk of his head. Isaac dropped his plate and cup into the tub and walked out.

Joe Sample silently watched a line of clouds build in the north. Lightning played along the horizon, though it was so far away there was no rumbling of thunder. "If that thing moves in, everybody'll have to stand extra guard tonight."

Isaac nodded. In a cowcamp, men developed a fatalistic attitude toward sleep; they knew they were not likely to get much of it, and they accepted this as a fact of life.

Joe Sample said, "Runyan hasn't given up. I think he would of left while ago if he hadn't had to leave here the loser. He's got no intention of leavin' this outfit till he's beaten you one way or the other."

"I don't want to fight him, but it looks like he's bound and determined to make me. I wisht you hadn't stepped in while ago, Joe. By now maybe him and me'd have it over with."

"I was tryin' to protect you."

Resentment came up unbidden. "You don't think I can protect myself?"

Joe Sample gave him a hard study. "I always been your friend, Isaac. I always will be if you let me. But you got to understand that there's some things you just can't do; you better let your friends do them for you."

"I could beat Pete Runyan if ever it come to that."

Sample frowned. "Maybe you could and maybe you couldn't. The point is, you better not. You still got friends in this outfit. Fight Pete Runyan, and I may be the only one you have left."

Angrily Isaac said, "You mean stay in my place and let my friends do my fightin' for me?"

"That's about it. There's some things you can't change."

Isaac made no reply to that. Anger flashed inside him as he watched the distant lightning.

Joe said, "Maybe the best idea is for me to send you back to the ranch first thing in the mornin'."

"If I leave here, then I'm the loser and Pete Runyan wins. Anyway, you don't have one man too many to get this herd where the Major needs it on time."

"If you and Pete fight, I'm liable to lose two men instead of one."

"I won't fight him, Joe, not unless he makes me. I'll stay out of his way."

"All right, Isaac, I'll hold you to that. Sometimes it takes a braver man to keep the peace than it does to fight."

Chapter Nine

They all stood double guard that night. The storm moved close but never quite reached them. Isaac rode slowly around the herd, talking to the cattle and keeping an eye on the distant lightning. The steers had been walked hard and were tired, but they had enough energy to run if anything gave them enough of a fright.

But daylight came and they were still on the bedground. Sleepy-eyed, Isaac took his breakfast and assumed his place on the point while the rest of the men roused the herd and got it started moving. A hard rain came an hour or so after sunup, enough to make him put on his yellow slicker. The sun broke through the clouds while the rain still fell. Isaac took that as a sign it would rain again tomorrow. It was a firm cowboy belief that when it rained with the sun shining it would rain again the next day; somebody had told him once that this knowledge came from the Indians.

Well, the more rain, the better the grass would be. But it did make things uncomfortable for a bunch of men driving cattle. He would rather have watched it from inside a dry barn.

The day passed with little incident. Isaac kept a good watch on the horizon for strange riders but saw none. The heavy gray clouds had broken up, but they still floated around, promising to regroup and rebuild. About the middle of the afternoon Joe Sample loped up to him and asked if he was doing all right.

"Fine," Isaac nodded. "A little fuzzy-headed from missin' sleep."

"So's everybody else. These cattle ought to be tired enough tonight not to run, and everybody can get a little more rest. But I'd like to see Hackamore Creek behind us first."

"You reckon it's on a rise?"

"Looks to me like it rained a right smart more to the north, where the creek heads up. I'm ridin' on ahead to take a look."

Isaac hadn't thought about Hackamore Creek; this was a piece of country with which he was only vaguely familiar. Being a ranchhand rather than a trail hand, he had not learned to anticipate problems like that. Now, because Joe had brought it up, Isaac found himself worrying.

After a while Joe came back. Isaac saw the grim look on his face and asked him no foolish questions. Joe said, "It's risin', and it's fixin' to get a good deal worse before it improves any. If we don't get across there this evenin' we're apt to be stuck on this side two–three days."

"The Major ain't got two–three days."

"Right. We're fixin' to push them like hell, Isaac. I'll bet you two bits we run over you."

"Bet you two bits you don't."

He didn't know where the strength came from, but the cowboys got those steers moved up into a trot, so Isaac had to make his fresh horse strike a long trot alongside the leaders.

He knew Hackamore Creek in its upper reaches, but this was a little south of his accustomed country. It was bigger here, fed by several springs downstream from where he knew it best. It was not far short of sundown when he topped a long rise and came in sight of the cottonwood-lined bank. He heard a horse loping up behind him and saw Joe Sample. Behind Joe a short way came Pete Runyan, from the left swing. Joe beckoned with his chin. "Let's go down and look at her, Isaac."

Isaac didn't like it. High water had always made his stomach tighten a little. He looked down at the angry creek. "Is it still risin'?"

Joe Sample said, "It's up from what it was while ago. I expect there's a lot of push yet to come. Best thing is to never let them cattle slow down; just run them the hell off in there before they have time to know what's happenin' to them."

Isaac pointed. "Bank's pretty steep on the other side. Climbin' out might be as bad as swimmin' across. Reckon there's an easier place up or down the stream?"

"I rode it while ago for a mile in each direction. We ain't got time to hunt further than that. One place is about as bad as another."

Isaac remained where he was, on the bank of the creek. The longer he looked down at that swirling brown water, the less he liked the whole situation. But they sure didn't have time to build a bridge. He watched Joe ride back to the herd and give orders. He caught sight of Wash's wagon, the tarp cover bobbing up and down. Wash would throw a conniption fit when he saw what he had to cross. Probably the best thing was to do with Wash what they had to do with the cattle: run him the hell off in there before he had a chance to think about it.

No, of course that wasn't practical. It would probably lose Wash and the wagon too. While he waited, Isaac rode up the creek a little way. Shortly he found trunks of two dead trees. He pitched his rope over them and dragged them one at a time to the top of the bank. These could be lashed to either side of the wagon for flotation.

As the cattle approached, Joe signaled for Isaac to hold them up. The foreman loped around, his horse's hoofs slinging blobs of mud. He motioned for Isaac and Pete Runyan and Hunter Proffitt, riding right swing, to come to him.

"I've told the other boys," Joe said. "We're goin' to let the drags come up a little more, then Isaac will ride off into that water and the rest of us will push a bunch of those cattle down that bank in a hard run, right behind him. If we get some started across, the rest ought to follow."

Pete Runyan smiled coldly at Isaac. "You a good swimmer, boy?"

Isaac swallowed. "I reckon I'll make it."

Runyan stared hard at him, dark humor in his eyes. "I can take your place, boy, if you're scared."

If anyone else had made that suggestion, Isaac

would have accepted it. Instead he said, "You ready, Mister Joe?"

Joe nodded. "Anytime."

Isaac stepped down and loosened his cinch a little to give the horse more freedom in swimming. He remounted, said, "I'll see you on the other side," and spurred down that rain-slippery bank, hitting the water in a run.

He didn't know how good a river horse this dun might be; he had never tested him at it. In fact, Isaac had never tested himself on a swollen river but a time or two. The churning water slammed against the horse with more force than Isaac expected. When he felt the animal floundering, Isaac slipped quickly out of the saddle and into the cold water. The sudden chill of it took his breath away, and the crushing force was greater than he had anticipated. He floated free, holding onto the horse's mane and the saddlehorn. He caught a mouthful of muddy water and choked as it went down the wrong pipe.

His eyes burned from the grit in the water, but he could see the cattle spilling over the bank and plunging into the creek behind him. He caught another mouthful of water and choked again, worse this time. He lost his hold on the saddlehorn and tightened what grip he still had on the mane. In a moment of sudden panic he could feel the water tugging at him like some malevolent animal, trying to drag him away. He clutched desperately at the horse, knowing that if he ever lost his hold he would die in this creek.

He felt the horse's feet take hold of solid ground. Isaac blinked away the burning mud as best he could and saw the opposite bank quickly coming up at him. He felt the ground under his own feet—soft mud, anyway—and knew he had made it across. He grabbed at the leather reins so the horse would not climb up the bank and run away from him. He scrambled up on his hands and knees, sinking to his wrists in spots in the mud, but when he got to the top he still had the reins.

Behind him he could hear the cowboys shout as they kept pushing steers off into the water. The first of the cattle were coming up on the bank now, following in the tracks of Isaac and his dun horse. The spotted lead steer went down on its knees, and another steer passed by it, surging, struggling against the steep bank. The spotted steer got to its feet and made an upward lunge, coming clear. Mud clung to its legs in an oblong ball, all the way to the knees.

Isaac realized that he had as much mud on himself as the steer did. He lifted the slicker and rubbed some off his hands and arms onto his pantslegs. His horse was still breathing hard from the exertion, as the steers did when they clambered up onto the east bank. Isaac retightened his cinch and swung into the saddle to push these cattle clear so they would not be a barrier against the others still in the water.

He saw Joe Sample's head as Joe's horse neared the top of the bank. He saw the horse's head and shoulders. Then, suddenly, the horse lost its footing in the mud and fell back. Isaac heard a cry of surprise from Joe, and heard some cowboy shout in alarm. Isaac jabbed spurs into his horse's ribs, rushing back to help.

He piled out of the saddle before his horse came to a stop, and he started down the bank in a rush. He could see Joe's horse most of the way down to the water, helplessly floundering, its legs in the air. He could see Joe's arm sticking out from beneath the horse, waving frantically.

Pete Runyan was closer than Isaac; he was just coming up out of the water. Runyan let his own horse go and made a rush afoot up the slope.

In his fright and concern, Isaac yelled needlessly at Runyan as he slipped and slid down the bank. "Help him, Runyan. For God's sake, get him out from under there."

Runyan had hold of the horse's reins, and he was trying to pull the animal up enough that it could get some purchase with its feet. Joe's horse had just begun to find some control and get clear of Joe when Runyan's own feet slipped from under him in the mud. The horse went back down on top of Joe, and Runyan on top of the horse.

Isaac got there just then. He grabbed Pete Runyan's arm and jerked the cowboy up, flinging him to one side.

He shouted, "Get out of the way, you clumsy son-of-a-bitch!" He got on the other side of Joe's horse and put himself where he could push against the horse's shoulder, to help it to its feet. Runyan found his own feet and caught the reins, pulling to add his own strength.

The horse managed to get up this time. A steer, clambering up the bank, almost ran over the prostrate Joe Sample. Isaac put himself on Joe's near side and caught with his shoulder the kick of a cloven hoof that might otherwise have struck Joe.

Joe's horse got its footing and struggled up the bank. Pete Runyan stood with chest heaving, looking down at Isaac and the wagonboss. Isaac demanded roughly, "Goddammit, what're you waitin' for? Help me get him up from here."

He knew when he put his hand beneath Joe's leg that he had done the wrong thing. Joe cried out in agony. The leg was broken.

Hunter Proffitt had made the bank and cut through the cattle to help. A couple of other cowboys also had come up. Together, carefully as they could in the slippery mud, they carried Joe up to the top, away from danger of being trampled by the cattle. Isaac took off his slicker and spread it on the ground, and they placed Joe on it. Joe's face was going gray. Shock was setting in.

Isaac said, "You'll be all right, Mister Joe. We've made it."

Joe gritted. "The cattle?"

Hunter Proffitt told him, "They're about all across."

Joe cursed mightily at the pain, as if he could drive it away. Isaac looked up from Joe's contorted face and into the brittle eyes of Pete Runyan. Runyan said, "I hope you was talkin' to that horse while ago."

Isaac knew he might sidestep trouble by saying that he was. A man might forgive hard words spoken in the pressure of the moment like that. But stubbornly he said, "No, I was talkin' to *you*."

"I believe you called me a son-of-a-bitch."

Isaac felt a chill coming over him; there wasn't a square inch of his hide that was not wet. "I believe that's what I said."

Joe Sample loosed a fresh string of profanity. "Goddamn the both of you! Ain't you got anything better to do than stand there and argue? We got the cattle to finish crossin'. We got to bring that chuckwagon over. First one of you that lays a hand on the other, I'll shoot him!"

Pete Runyan backed off, his eyes narrowed. "He's right, boy. But when we're done, me and you have got a right smart to talk about."

As strawboss, Hunter Proffitt took over without any questions. He assigned Alf Train to stand by Joe Sample. He sent Pete Runyan and most of the other cowboys to see after getting the herd back a safe distance from the creek, in case it should yet get out of its banks, and to bed the cattle down for the night. He beckoned Isaac and Chalk Denson and another to recross the river with him and get the chuckwagon. Isaac did not relish going over again, but he asked no favors; somebody had to do it.

They lashed the dead logs to the wagon, then each horseman tied one end of his rope to it and dallied the other end to his saddlehorn. With these ropes as anchorage so the current would not carry the vehicle away, they floated it across. The hardest part was in getting the wagon up the steep bank, every cowboy tying on and adding the strength of his own horse to the struggle.

Wash sat up on the wagonseat through it all, handling his own lines. He was more than frightened, but he did not quail from the task or make complaint. Isaac felt a grudging admiration for the old man and wondered if he had judged him too harshly.

Carefully they picked up Joe Sample and lifted him onto the wagon, then took it to a point beyond the floodplain where Wash could safely make camp. It took several extra ropes and horsemen pulling to get the wheels through the soft mud.

At length Proffitt said, "Wash, we done all we can do. The rest of it is up to you."

Wash forced a smile. "You-all done real well, Mister Hunter."

Isaac gritted his teeth. Somehow the way Wash said *Mister* sort of spoiled it. Wash was able to make himself face that angry creek, but he wasn't going to assert any equality with these men he had known so long, men he should have been able to count as his friends.

While they waited for Wash to get supper ready, Pete Runyan and Isaac and Hunter Proffitt set Joe's broken leg the best they could and splinted it with a cottonwood limb. Joe had drunk a good part of a bottle he carried in his warbag against such an emergency. Hunter said, "It ain't but ten—twelve miles to the Lockridge ranch headquarters. After supper I'll send Isaac to fetch back a spring wagon for you, Joe. You've gone as far on this drive as you're goin'."

Joe cursed, as much in self-anger as in pain. "Goddamn fool thing to let happen."

"Wasn't no way you could help it."

"You didn't see anybody else break *his* leg, did you? Just me. First time the Major ever had such a desperate need, and I pull a damnfool stunt like this!"

"We'll make it all right, Joe," Hunter said confidently. "You already got us over the roughest part, the startin'."

Joe looked up first at Pete Runyan, then at Isaac. "I don't know that I have. Looks to me like there's two bigger fools on this trip than even *I* am."

Hunter said, "Joe, I was thinkin' it'd be a smart thing if I was to send Isaac with you back to town."

Isaac protested. "You need everybody you've got if you're goin' to get them cattle there on time."

Joe said, "Hunter's right, Isaac. I heard what you said to Pete while I was under that horse. It wasn't really called for."

Isaac looked at the cowboys gathered in a circle. He saw reproach in the eyes of many. Word had gotten around, and they were siding with Runyan.

Isaac knew he had spoken harshly and out of turn. But it had been building in him, and he had said it, and now he wouldn't take it back for two hundred dollars. He chewed his lip and cast about for an argument that would hold water. "Whatever trouble me and Pete Runyan have got, *I'm* man enough to put it aside till we get this job over with."

Runyan shrugged. "I reckon I can set it on the shelf too, till we've got this thing done for the Major."

Joe Sample studied both men critically, and with anger. "What *then*? You goin' to kill one another?"

No answer came from either man. Joe Sample took another long drag at his bottle, his face twisting harshly. "Hell's bells, maybe you *ought* to. I ain't had so much grief over *nothin'* since the big war."

Chapter Ten

It was way into the night when Isaac got back with the spring wagon from the Lockridge ranch, and big Sam Lockridge came with him to take care of Joe. Several of them helped put Joe in the wagon. The wagon was out of Isaac's sight before it had gone thirty yards, but he stood awhile listening to the rattle of trace chains and the loose sideboards as it went away. Regret was heavy on Isaac, not only for Joe Sample but for himself. Joe was the best friend he had in camp.

Hunter Proffitt said, "You better get what sleep you can, Isaac. You'll be standin' guard after a while, and we got a hard day again tomorrow." He said it with the firmness of a boss.

"Yes sir," Isaac said, sensing that things had tightened up. He went back to his blankets.

His was the last guard duty, so he was among the last to eat. The rest of the men were catching up their horses while he bolted his breakfast. As they rode out to the herd, Hunter Proffitt moved alongside Pete Runyan. "Pete, I want you to take the left point." He turned back, his eyes seeking Isaac. "Isaac, you'll take Pete's place on the left swing."

The order hit Isaac as hard as a clenched fist. He made no reply, and Hunter asked, "Isaac, did you hear me?"

Isaac made himself nod. "Yes sir, I hear you." There was no way he could have hidden his disappointment, even if he had tried to. Proffitt turned away from him, and pretty soon he was on the far side of the herd, getting the steers to their feet.

Pete Runyan looked back at Isaac. Isaac avoided his eyes; he didn't know if the cowboy was gloating or not.

I ought to've gone with Joe Sample, he told himself, the bitterness coming up like brine in a bad spring. *Damn him, Runyan's beaten me anyway.*

Isaac nursed his anger, keeping it banked, not hot enough to get in the way of the work he had to do, but purposely prodding it enough to keep it from dying away and going cold. He ate little at noon, keeping to his accustomed wagontongue and turning his back so that more than ever before he sat alone. He looked no one in the eye but had an uncomfortable feeling that everybody was watching him, perhaps agreed that he had it coming, that Hunter Proffitt had put him in his proper place.

He hadn't spoken six unnecessary words to anybody in six days. Day after day he rode along doing his job, often staring at Pete Runyan way ahead. His sense of injustice had not diminished; on the contrary, it had chewed at him, feeding on itself and growing like a cancer until his stomach was so upset that he had a hard time holding anything in it. He ate enough to sustain himself, but no more.

Nobody had much to say to him, either. He sensed that he had raised a barrier of sorts, and at times he had moments of regret for that. Other times he told himself simply, *The hell with them. If they like Pete Runyan so damned much, let them have him.*

They pushed the cattle hard, giving them too little time to graze as they needed to. Like Isaac, they ate just enough to hold themselves together. Isaac could see that the steers were drawing some. They were tired, but they were also edgier than they had been in the beginning. Given reason, they could cause trouble.

The first rain had passed over, but now another storm was coming up from the north. All afternoon Isaac watched it build on the horizon, moving closer, getting darker and meaner-looking. By supper the thunder was starting to roll, though still at some distance. Hunter Proffitt called for double guard duty.

By midnight the clouds had moved in, and the lightning was near enough to throw an occasional flash of illumination across the prairie. The north wind brought a chilly dampness and a vague smell of rain. Isaac heard someone up stirring around quietly and in a flash of lightning recognized Hunter Proffitt walking toward his horse. Isaac raised up on one elbow and listened to Hunter riding off in the direction of the herd. Directly he was back, calling for more men. He said some of the cattle were on their feet and plenty nervous.

Isaac had been sleeping with his clothes on, as usual. Grudgingly he laid back the tarp and the top blanket. A drop of water hit him in the face. Sprinkling. This country always did seem to need one more rain, but he had as soon it didn't come in the middle of the dark night while he was standing guard.

He put on his hat, then pulled his boots from under the protection of the tarp and tugged and stamped them onto his feet. Moving to the fire, he saw Wash huddled there half asleep, a blanket pulled around him. Wash had gotten up to make extra coffee and never had gone back to bed. Wash stirred, saw who was at his coffeepot, and glanced back over his shoulder to see if anyone else was up and around yet.

"Isaac, how come you here?"

"Hunter called for more guards."

"I mean how come you still with this drive? You ought to've gone back with Joe Sample and got clear of this trouble."

"I don't see no trouble."

"The hell you don't. You been about as cheerful as a wounded badger. I wish to hell you'd gone home."

"If I had, it would've been like sayin' Pete Runyan had beaten me."

"Well, ain't he? What's wrong with gettin' beat now and again? You been beaten before. You're still livin'; you're still healthy."

"Sure I been beaten before. But all of a sudden I've taken to askin' myself why. Why put up with it? Why not fight back? I'm as good a man in my worst day as Pete Runyan ever was in his best."

"I don't have to tell you there's one big difference."

"No, you *don't* have to tell me. All of a sudden I've got real tired of puttin' up with *that*, too."

Acidly Wash said, "You fixin' to find some way to wash yourself white?"

Isaac blew on the coffee and decided against even attempting an answer.

Wash said, "You was just a boy when slavery come to a stop, so you don't know all there was about it. But me, I was a man growed. There was a time I had some of the same notions you got now, only I learned better. I got the whip scars all over my back to show how good I learned."

"That was a different time."

"You think it was? It ain't so different. You step over the line and you'll find out real quick it ain't so different. You'll find out like I did that when all the hol-lerin' is over with and them bluebelly soldiers is gone home, you still ain't nothin' but a nigger."

Lightning flashed close in, and a sharp clap of thun-der shook the tin cups and plates in the chuckbox. Isaac pitched out what was left of the coffee and handed the wet, dripping cup to Wash. "*You* can go on and be a nigger all your life if you want to, but Isaac Jefford is a *man*!"

The rain was slashing down at him by the time he reached the herd, beating hard against his yellow slicker. The lightning flashes came so frequently that one seemed to linger almost to the next. Many steers were on their feet, stirring restlessly. Isaac decided at a glance that it was not a question of whether they would run . . . the question was how long it would be before they started.

He began riding in a circle around the herd, meeting other riders moving in the opposite direction. He talked to the cattle. "Now, boys, you settle down now. Ain't nothin' to it but a little storm, and it'll pass. You don't see ol' Isaac flinchin' none, do you?" He talked to let them hear the sound of his voice. "Now, boys, you ain't fixin' to run. Wherever you go, it'll be the same as here. Settle down and take your rest, and the sun'll be up in the mornin'."

He talked as much for himself as for the cattle. He

had no great fear of storms, but still they always made him uneasy; they made him feel helpless and small in the manifestation of all that terrible power. The bright flashes hurt his eyes, and they brought back a grisly memory of a cowboy who had foolishly sought shelter from the rain by riding under a lone tree. The bolt had even melted his spurs.

The one that brought the herd to its feet struck somewhere nearby. The blinding flash brought Isaac's hands to his face and left him blinking at the pain in his eyes. A second after the flash came a thunderclap, as loud as if Isaac had held his ear against a cannon. He heard the sudden rattle of hoofs and knew the cattle were on the run. For a confused, flash-blinded moment he grabbed at the horn and simply tried to stay in the saddle as the horse instinctively broke into a run with the cattle. Opening his eyes, he saw nothing except the lingering flash, burned on the retina. He gripped with his knees and gave slack on the reins, having to trust the horse until his vision cleared. He could hear the splash and splatter of all those hoofs on the muddy ground.

As sight came, the continuing lightning showed him he was near the lead of the running cattle. So far as he could tell, no other rider was ahead of him. He could hear others behind him, shouting against the pounding hoofs and the clatter of striking horns and the crashing thunder.

There was little point in trying to stop or turn cattle in the first moments of a run like this; they were usually so panicked that they would trample anything which got in their way. After they had run awhile and fatigue began to set in, a man had a chance to gain some control. It was hard to tell in this darkness and this driving rain, but Isaac thought they were running in an easterly direction. That was one point to the good, at least; they weren't wasting all this travel.

He kept touching spurs to the horse's ribs to let him edge closer to the lead, keeping well to the side so that if the horse fell he wouldn't do it in front of all those cattle. Isaac had never seen a man killed by a stampede, but he had heard stories. Even allowing for exaggeration, they were bad enough.

The horse's hoofs struck something solid, and Isaac knew they had come suddenly upon an outcrop of rock in what had been a rolling prairie. Fear stabbed him as he felt the horse stumble on the slick rocks, go down almost to his knees, then catch his footing. He looked back and saw, in a momentary flash, the dark bobbing outline of those cattle behind him.

Then the horse slipped again, and Isaac's heart jumped. This time he was going down. He kicked his feet free of the stirrups to avoid being hung to the saddle. He knew the sickening sensation of falling. He landed first on his left shoulder, sharp rocks cutting into his flesh like a grater shredding corn into meal. His head struck ground, and he saw a blinding flash that was not lightning. He lay stunned, knowing the horse was threshing to find its feet. Isaac realized the cattle behind him were likely to come running over him, their sharp hoofs beating him into the ground. He struggled to pull himself up, his fingers clutching desperately for something solid he could hold to.

The lightning showed a big, dark figure looming over him, and he ducked instinctively, expecting to be struck. A rider swung down quickly from a horse and grabbed Isaac beneath the armpits, pulling him to his feet. He thrust Isaac forward, and Isaac felt rather than saw his own horse, his empty saddle.

A voice said calmly, "Don't be a-layin' down on the job, Isaac." The voice was Pete Runyan's.

Isaac somehow found his stirrup with his left foot and felt Runyan giving him a quick boost up. Isaac landed in the saddle and jammed his right boot into its stirrup. Cattle were rushing by on both sides of him. He held his ground, giving Runyan momentary protection while Runyan swung back onto his own horse.

Isaac was still stunned. He held the horn and gave the horse its head, trusting it to find its own way out of this mess. The horse, as frightened as Isaac had been, immediately rammed into Runyan's mount and came dangerously near knocking it off its feet.

"Watch out," Runyan shouted. "I didn't come here to trade places with you."

Then they were running again, after the cattle. Isaac

felt a sharp pain in his side as the saddle pounded against his rump, and he wondered if he might have broken a rib. The driving rain hit him in the face. He realized for the first time that he had lost his hat. His cheek burned like fire, the mud running into a wound cut by a sharp rock as he had fallen.

He had no idea how far the cattle had run, and at the moment he didn't give a damn. Gradually he could tell that the cattle were slowing down. Their legs and their wind would only let them run so far, and even panic must give way eventually to weariness.

He decided because they were going in more or less the right direction anyway, the best idea was to let them run themselves out. If he tried to turn them, they might run awhile in the wrong direction and have all that distance to make up tomorrow. Gradually the steers eased from a hard run to an easy one, and then to a long trot, and finally to a walk. Most hung their heads now, near exhaustion. Isaac moved up in front of them and began shouting, bringing them to a halt, turning them back against each other so that those in front served as a barrier against those bringing up the rear. Pete Runyan joined him. In a little while they had the cattle stopped, and Isaac began looking behind him for other cowboys.

The cattle they had were nowhere near the entire herd. In the flashes of lightning he tried to make some sort of estimate. He thought there might be three or four hundred head. Somewhere in the run the cattle had split up. It dawned on him presently that he and Pete Runyan were by themselves.

For some odd reason the first outside thought to break into his mind was of Alvin Quain and that band of robbers. Wouldn't Quain like to catch him out here, isolated? But Isaac knew this was a foolish notion. A robber would have sense enough to hole up somewhere and not poke his head out in a storm like this; only a cowboy was so dumb as to expose himself to the elements and get himself knocked half senseless and soaked and cold and hungry.

With each flash of lightning he looked for sign of anybody else, and as the momentary light faded he felt growing disappointment. It occurred to him that these cattle were tired enough now that they wouldn't drift far even if he left them to go hunt the rest of the bunch. But he dismissed the idea. He had only a vague notion where he was, and if he left these cattle in the dark he might not find them again. A rain like this from now to daylight wouldn't leave enough tracks to follow. He might not even find anyone else; he might simply wind up lost.

He glanced at Pete Runyan, riding toward him from the other side of their small herd. *That'd tickle Runyan,* he thought darkly, *me gettin' lost and never comin' back.*

Runyan asked, "You all right, Isaac? Any bones broke?"

Isaac had already felt his ribs and decided nothing had been broken; he was probably bruised to the core, though. Crisply he responded, "Would it make any difference if there was?"

"Sure. You wouldn't be much help; I'd wind up doin' the work."

Isaac decided that was indeed the only thing Runyan was worried about. Reluctantly he said, "I reckon I ought to thank you for pickin' me up."

Runyan shrugged. "It was so dark I didn't know who it was, at first."

"If you'd known it was me, would you of stopped?"

Runyan looked at him calmly in the bluish flash of lightning, arms straight and braced against his saddlehorn. "I can't rightfully say."

Well, thought Isaac, *you got to give him one thing. He's honest.*

Isaac turned away and left Runyan to ride slowly around the cattle. He knew the only sensible thing was to stay right here and watch over these steers until daybreak, and hope that elsewhere other cowboys were doing the same. Maybe if he kept his back turned, he could pretend Pete Runyan wasn't here.

The fall had lacerated his slicker on the left side and had flared it open so that the rain had driven in. Isaac was soaked to the hide. Now the wind took on an icy breath; from the feel of it he knew there was hail somewhere nearby. He sat shivering, remembering that half cup of hot coffee he had thrown away just before he rode out to the herd. Right now he would trade a good pocketknife and maybe a rope to boot, just to have it back.

To the tired steers he said sourly, "Now boys, ain't you ashamed of yourselves, actin' like a bunch of cattle?"

Daylight brought him no particular comfort aside from the fact that he could see better. He was still cold, and his whole left side was in pain, from his rock-cut cheek to his knee. He had no real idea how far he was from where the run had started—three or four miles, at least. During the run he had felt the cattle were traveling generally eastward, but now he wasn't even sure about that. Not one landmark showed on the prairie that he could tie to.

The thunder and lightning had passed on southward, leaving only the rain. That fell gentler now. The wind had eased, but Isaac shivered. He had no coat with him; normally at this time of year a coat was excess baggage. He wished the sun would break out, but he saw no sign of it through the leaden clouds.

He had avoided Pete Runyan, and Runyan had seemed to like it that way. But now with daylight, Runyan rode up to him. He looked at Isaac's torn slicker and at the wound on Isaac's face. Isaac thought he saw a flicker of sympathy, but on a second look he guessed he was wrong. Runyan said, "Looks like you got somewhat the worst of it, boy."

Stubbornly Isaac said, "I've had a lot worse happen to me."

"All in all, I reckon you come out pretty lucky."

"If you're lookin' for me to thank you, I already done that."

"Your thanks never entered into my thinkin'."

Isaac tried to control his shivering, for he thought it made him weak in Runyan's eyes. But he could not stop it. Runyan said, "Nothin' dry enough to make a fire with, so I reckon all you can do is shiver yourself warm. You hungry?"

Isaac was, but his pride kept him from showing it. "I'm doin' just fine."

Runyan reached beneath his slicker, working a jackknife and a plug of tobacco out of his britches pocket. He pared off a sizable sliver of tobacco and raised it to his mouth with the point of the blade. "It's no substitute for beef and biscuits, but it does help take the edge off of a man's hunger. You care for a chew?"

"I never chewed tobacco," Isaac said.

"There comes a time for learnin' everything."

"I'm doin' just fine."

Runyan shrugged and turned his horse around, riding off to the other side of the scattered cattle. Isaac turned the opposite direction, putting Pete Runyan out of sight if not out of mind. He considered riding back to look for the rest of the outfit but decided that was needless. Sooner or later the others would come up to him and Runyan.

He could see now that the rain had not washed out all the signs. Where the tracks were gone, the trampled grass still gave plentiful evidence where the cattle had run.

About mid-morning he saw a familiar sight, Hunter Proffitt's big gray horse plodding along as Hunter followed the trail by the hoof-punished grass. Pete Runyan rode around from the far side of the loose-herded cattle so that he was near Isaac when Proffitt reached them. Proffitt was carrying something on his saddle. He held it out toward Isaac. "Found this a good ways back yonder. I expect it's yours."

It was Isaac's hat, a shapeless mass of sodden felt, streaked by mud. There was a hole in the top which he figured had been made by a hoof.

Hunter said, "Didn't find you under it, Isaac, so I figured you made it through all right." He saw the raw wound on Isaac's face and cast a quick, questioning glance at Runyan.

Runyan said, "It wasn't me. He taken a bad fall."

Isaac thanked Proffitt for the hat and set about trying to put some shape back into it. The water made it heavy and unnatural on his head.

Hunter turned to Runyan. "How many you got here, Pete?"

"I taken a rough count. I think there's about three hundred and twenty head."

Proffitt was pleased. "That accounts for most of

them, then. We're only out fifty or seventy-five. You done real good, Pete. Real good."

What about me? Isaac thought angrily. *I wasn't exactly sleepin' under the chuckwagon.*

Pete Runyan shrugged. "Just doin' what I'm paid for."

Chapter Eleven

Hunter Proffitt left Isaac to watch after the cattle and keep them from straying. He took Pete Runyan away, telling him he wanted him and three or four other men to scout and see if they might pick up any strays. Isaac watched them over the horizon, knowing Pete Runyan would manage to stop by Wash's wagon and get something to eat, long before Isaac could.

The first sign Isaac saw of the herd was Wash's wagon, slogging through the mud. Isaac decided the cattle wouldn't drift far, so he rode back to meet Wash, volunteering to help him make noon camp. "You got anything I could eat, Wash? I didn't have no breakfast."

"Neither did anybody else," Wash told him without sympathy. "They done et up what cold biscuits was left. Got nothin' now but cold beans. You can have some of them . . . *after* you've helped me set up to cook."

Isaac couldn't remember when cold beans had ever tasted so good, even without a biscuit or hot coffee.

Still smarting from Isaac's harsh words to him last night, Wash wouldn't put the coffeepot on until he judged that it was nearly time for the cowboys to ride in. Mostly Wash talked to himself, complaining about the hardship of having to cook with wet wood.

Eventually the rest of the herd showed up, minus the strays Pete Runyan had gone to look for. The cowboys left a skeleton crew and loped up to the wagon, as hungry as Isaac had been. Wash had the beans heated and some steak fried and hot biscuits browned in two Dutch ovens. Isaac almost wished now that he had waited, for the cold beans had taken the edge off his appetite.

Pete Runyan and the others came up with a few strays while Isaac was helping Wash load his wagon to move on. Runyan said something about going back to look for more, but Hunter Proffitt shook his head. "You-all done real fine. We need time more than we need whatever cattle are still out. Eat some dinner, then move up on the point, Pete. We'll be pushin' like hell from now on."

There was no question about it when they struck the big trail which the cow outfits used in driving north to the railroad. It was not a single trail; actually it was many trails running parallel, used so often that the hoofs had worn deep ruts into the ground where grass would not grow. Cattle moving northward would fall instinctively into the same paths used by their predecessors. They did not walk in straight lines, so the trails laced in and out like the veins in a green leaf, touching one another at angles, crossing over. The herds which came early in the spring usually got the grass, so the later herds would move farther and farther out to one side or the other, making the trail ever and ever wider.

Sunshine and warm wind had largely dried out the top moisture left by the rains. To the south Isaac could see dust, evidently stirred by a big herd on the trail where there was little or no grass to hold it down. Not knowing whether the Pierce herds already had passed or were still to the south, Hunter Proffitt sent one man north to overtake the last herd which had passed, one south to intercept the herd stirring all that dust. In an hour or so Isaac saw several riders coming up the trail from the south in a hard trot. One was Major Lytton.

We made it on time, he thought with relief.

Riding beside the Major was a bearded, incredibly tall man who seemed to be doing a lot of talking. His voice carried far across the prairie ahead of him. Isaac could hear this man's voice plainly and make out the words long before he could hear the Major's replies. Isaac had never seen Abel Head "Shanghai" Pierce, but he knew this had to be him. Pierce was known from the South Texas ranch country where he headquartered to the farthest trail town north where his herds went, and into the board rooms of many banks far beyond. He was noted for being loud and rough and profane, yet a man who kept his word. The third man of the four was Alf Train, whom Proffitt had sent south looking for the Major; it seemed when someone was chosen to ride off on an errand of some responsibility, it was usually Train. It must have been tiring, Isaac thought, but he got to see a lot of country.

The fourth man, Isaac noted with interest, was a Negro. He recalled stories that Pierce always had with him a Negro named Neptune as servant, bodyguard, and friend.

The more Isaac saw of the gangling Pierce, the more he stood in awe of him. He had never heard such a commanding voice. That hearty, far-reaching laugh could probably have stampeded a herd that was not yet trail-broken, he thought. Pierce and the Major had evidently arrived beforehand at some kind of price agreement based on description of the cattle. However, Isaac had never heard such a bellowing of profanity as Pierce contended that the cattle were not exactly as described. The wrangle and the quarrel went on for some time as Pierce tried for some extra concession. At fifty yards Isaac could hear all of Pierce's argument, very little of the Major's. At length Pierce agreed to a deal, with a condition.

"Like I been tellin' you all the way, it's too many cattle to throw in with my other herds. I'll want to keep this bunch separate. Now, by God, sir, if you want me to buy this herd off of you, you've got to let me buy your cowboys too."

The Major made some protest about needing the men, but Pierce was adamant. "I need your Goddamned crew. Without them, these Arkansas razorbacks you call steers ain't worth a hoot in hell to me. Now you got to take it or leave it, and I think you'll take it, sir. I got you where the hair is short."

The Major said reluctantly, "I'll need to keep two or three men. I have to get this money into Fort Worth."

Pierce rammed his huge paw forward, and Isaac could imagine he was crushing every bone in the Major's hand.

Pierce turned to the cowboys, those near enough to

be watching him. None were so far away they could not
hear him. "All right, by God, you're workin' for me now,
at least till we get these cattle to the railroad. Let's get
them strung out before the next herd comes up and starts
chewin' the burrs out of their tails."

Isaac's eyes narrowed as he watched the tall cow-
man gesturing. He decided he was a little afraid of Pierce,
and the idea of going up the trail with him filled Isaac
with dread. But a deal was a deal, and the Major had
made it. It wasn't as if it was going to last forever; it
wasn't like the days of slavery. Isaac waved his arm,
shouting at the steers.

He was so busy he didn't notice the Major come up
behind him. "Isaac," the Major said, "I need you. Come
along."

Isaac blinked, surprised but pleased. "I thought I
was goin' with Mister Pierce."

The Major shook his head. "Isaac, there is nothing
in Dodge City that you would care to see."

"No sir, there sure ain't." Isaac gratefully pulled his
horse around and followed. The Major asked him about
the mark on his face, and Isaac told him about the stampede.

The Major rode up to Hunter Proffitt, and Isaac figured Proffitt was the second man he would want to re-
serve. But the Major said, "Hunter, Shang is going to
need a good boss with this herd, so you're it. Work for
him just like you'd work for me, and when you-all get
finished with this drive you come on home and you'll be
working for me again."

Proffitt was pleased at the prospect of the trip. "You
got any special ideas how to get along with Shanghai
Pierce?"

"Just do the job the best you know how, and if he
doesn't like it you'll hear from him."

"That," Proffitt said, "I don't doubt for a minute."

They bottled up the herd, then began to let the cattle
move out in a thin line. Pierce and the Negro Neptune
each made a count as the cattle went by them. The Major
and Pete Runyan made a count for the Major's interests.
Each had a different method. Pierce carried a long rawhide thong. Each time he got to a hundred he tied a quick

knot in the thong and started the count over. Pete Runyan had a bunch of small stones in his left hand, and each time he reached a hundred he transferred one to his right hand. The final steer passed, a sore-footed paint with a freshly broken horn. The men compared their figures. Runyan's count was the highest, Pierce's the lowest, and the spread between them was only six. Pierce and the Major split the difference.

Pierce said, "Now you understand, Major, I'm only makin' this deal with you as an accommodation for old friendship. I had me a right smart of hell raisin' this much cash money on no notice. I ain't payin' you no extry for the use of your horses or your wagon. I'm just payin' your men their wages startin' tomorrow mornin'. Seein' as this day is two-thirds over, I take it as only fair that you pay them today."

The Major was itching to leave, and he wasn't going to break up a deal over details. He nodded but said, "Shang, I always heard that you had more brass than a courthouse cannon."

"It ain't me that's in trouble with the bank, sir," Pierce reminded him. "A man who don't take advantage of circumstances is goin' to find himself took advantage *of*. I've had to wear the left boot on my right foot more than once, and no son-of-a-bitch ever wept tears over me."

Pierce removed the bulging saddlebags from his horse and dropped them on the ground. They made a considerable thud. The Major untied the blankets from behind his own saddle and spread them out. The two men sat there like poker players and counted out greenbacks on those blankets. When they were done, the Major had most of them, but Pierce retained a fair wad.

"By rights," the Major said, "I ought to have the rest of that. You're getting these cattle cheap. They'll fetch you a nice profit at the railhead."

"It's a long ways to the railhead," Pierce reminded him loudly. "Ever Goddamned thing a man can imagine is up there in front of us . . . Indians, rustlers, fire, flood, famine. . . ."

The Major smiled wryly, for Pierce was spreading it

thick. "You never failed in your life to get a herd all the way to the railhead, usually bigger than when it started." That was a reference to a widespread trail driver tendency to pick up whatever strays presented themselves en route, if no one was around to call his hand. Many a man made his overhead on strays.

Pierce shoved his remaining greenbacks into his saddlebags. "A deal is a deal. I still don't see why you couldn't handle this with a bank draft. It'd be a lot less dangerous than carryin' the cash."

"The contract specifies cash, and Norris is a stickler for the terms of the contract when they're in his favor. I took him a draft once; he refused to accept it. He's trying to beat me out of my ranch, and he'll use every technicality he can find."

Pierce grunted. "Only difference between him and Captain Kidd was that Kidd used a ship. Norris works off of a marble-topped desk. But it's a long ways down when you walk the plank."

Neptune tied Pierce's saddlebags back onto his boss's saddle. Pierce turned for a final word. "How long did you say you got to get to Fort Worth?"

"The day after tomorrow," the Major said.

Pierce frowned. "Then you better not waste no time settin' here frettin' over how bad I skinned you. And Major . . ."

"Yes?"

"This is an ungodly lot of money you're carryin'. Them men that've trailed us since we left the bank, they'll be trailin' you now, I expect. If I was you I'd get set to run them one hell of a race."

"I had figured on taking all my men with me for protection."

"Sorry, Major, but I got my problems too. Good luck, sir."

Pierce and the Negro rode off, heading south toward their other cattle.

Isaac's eyes had widened some. "Major, what was that he said about somebody trailin' after you?"

The Major nodded soberly as he packed the greenbacks into his saddlebags. "Some or all of that bunch that killed Lon Whitten, I believe. They've got a fine nose for money."

Isaac swallowed. "Is Alvin Quain with them, you reckon?"

"They never got close enough that I could recognize anybody. But Quain must have known the financial trouble they left me in when they killed Lon. He probably figured out that I'd have to get more money in a hurry. My guess is that he and the others decided to follow me."

"Now they'll be after you the way they was after Lon Whitten."

"You scared, Isaac?"

"Sure I'm scared. But I'll go with you plumb to the North Pole if you want me to. All you got to do is ask."

"I know that, Isaac. And I've got a trip for you to make, but it won't be with me. It'll be with Pete Runyan."

Isaac's jaw dropped. Runyan was still close enough to hear, and he spilled half the coils of the rope he was tying to his saddlehorn. "What's this about me and Isaac?"

The Major pointed across the prairie to the west. "See anything over there?"

Isaac looked hard but saw nothing. Neither did Runyan.

The Major said, "He was there a little while ago, a man. My guess is that he had a spyglass, and he watched Shang and me count out the money."

Runyan touched the stock of his saddlegun. "If he's out there, it'd be an easy matter to go get him."

"He can see you better than you can see him. He'd kill you before you got close. And even if you got him, I am sure there are others waiting somewhere just out of sight." The Major patted the saddlebags. "They're after what I have here. It'll be up to you and Isaac to see that they don't get it."

Runyan frowned at Isaac. "You got a dozen good men with this outfit, Major. Why him?"

Anger brought a question boiling from Isaac. "And why *him*?"

The Major's gaze shifted from one to another without acknowledging the antagonism between the two men. "Pete, there's a lot you don't know about Isaac, and I don't have the time right now to explain it all. I'll just tell you that toward the end of the war I was wounded . . . grievously wounded. I had Isaac with me then as a servant. He could have run off and left me anytime, and nobody would have known, or much cared. He would've been much safer if he *had*, because the war was still being fought all around us. But Isaac stayed and took care of me and got me onto my feet. Then he took me home. It was hell . . . more hell than you can imagine. But he stayed by me, and he's stayed by me ever since. Now, if it's his color that offends you, that's too bad. It's your fault and not his. Isaac Jefford is the best man I've got."

Runyan's eyes hadn't softened any that Isaac could tell. "He's already admitted that he's afraid."

"He was afraid during the war, too. So was I. But he never backed away."

Isaac said, "Major, if Runyan don't want to go, we don't need him. There's other men in this outfit six times better than he is."

"Not for *this* job, Isaac. I've got a lot of good cowboys, but for this job I need more than that."

Runyan put in. "You said we wouldn't be goin' with you. How can we protect you if we're not with you? You can't get that money to Fort Worth by yourself."

"I'm not going to," the Major replied. "*You* are. That is, Isaac will protect the money and you'll protect Isaac."

Disappointment touched Isaac; this was the first time the Major had ever sent him on a dangerous errand and had not gone himself. Isaac caught a look in Runyan's eyes that told him Runyan was thinking the same.

The Major said, "I'll take Alf Train with me. We'll start right away and decoy them. It's natural for them to think I have the money and come after us. You two will stay with the herd until good dark, then you'll take out for Fort Worth."

Isaac felt ashamed of his momentary doubt. It appeared to him that the Major was taking the real risk. "They won't wait to see if you really got the money, Major. They'll kill you first."

"They'll have to catch us, and I have no intention of letting them do that. Alf and I will take the fastest horses we have, and we'll hit a long run when we leave here. It's not far across to the Circle Dot ranch headquarters, and a lot of cowboys. We'll hole up there with all that protection for the night. The robbers will sit and wait for us to leave in the morning. But we won't leave. We'll sit and they'll sit. And while we're all sitting, you'll be on your way to Fort Worth."

It sounded good, Isaac would have to admit. All but his having to ride with Pete Runyan.

Runyan said, "Even if we don't have *that* bunch on our tail, somebody else might get an idea."

The Major shook his head. "Who would suspect you're carrying money? Look at Isaac . . . no stranger is going to figure he has three dollars in his pocket. As for you, Pete, no offense meant, but you've got *cowboy* written all over you, from the top of that old hat to that wornout pair of boots. Nobody's going to figure you've got money to pay a stable fee for your horse."

Runyan nodded slowly. "But you're still puttin' a lot of faith in *us*. How do you know you can trust us? How do you know Isaac won't take all your money and run off with it, or that *I* won't?"

"Isaac has carried money for me before, even if never this much. I know him. As for you, Pete, I've always prided myself on being a judge of character. There are lots of things you might do to a man, but rob or betray him is one thing you wouldn't. And anyway . . ." the Major paused, a humorless smile touching his face and then quickly gone, "anyway, if you tried it, Isaac Jefford would kill you dead!"

Runyan glanced at Isaac, and Isaac made sure the man saw his face at its hardest. Runyan said, "I got a feelin' he might do that even if I *didn't* try anything."

The Major turned to Isaac. "You know how important this is, Isaac. I want you to put your feelings aside. If you don't think you can, tell me now."

"You know me and Runyan don't even agree on what color the sky is. If I didn't go, what would you do, Major?"

"Maybe send someone else. More likely, I'd take Alf and Pete and the money and the three of us make a run for it. Maybe we'd get there, and maybe we wouldn't. The thing is, you know the way to Fort Worth, and the places to stop for horses. And when you get there, you know how to find J. Warren Norris without losing any time. I need you, Isaac."

Isaac looked at the ground. "You always grab a man where the hair is short, Major. You know I ain't never turned you down." He raised his eyes to Pete Runyan. "One thing I want to know: is he boss over me on this trip?"

The Major pondered that a minute; the question had not occurred to him. "I'll split the responsibility between you. Isaac, you're the boss over the money, and over getting it to Fort Worth on time. The bags will be on your saddle. Pete is the boss if you run into trouble; he knows how to handle that kind of situation." He looked at Runyan. "That suit you all right?"

Runyan said, "I never took orders from no dark-complected gentleman."

"Consider them *my* orders, not his."

Runyan frowned. "Seems to me like I ought to have a bonus comin' when this is over, seein' what I got to go through."

"All right. A dangerous job deserves a bonus, I suppose."

"It ain't the danger; looks to me like *you're* the one takin' on the danger. It's bumpin' stirrups with Isaac Jefford all the way to Fort Worth that's beyond the call of duty."

The Major showed a flash of impatience. "If I had anybody else, I do believe I'd put *both* of you to bringing up the drags for Shanghai Pierce." He suppressed the anger. "If you'll get the money there on time, and not kill each other, you'll *both* earn a bonus. Now, Isaac, you tie these bags onto your saddle and hang onto them like they were your very life. Because they *are*!"

Shortly the Major and Alf Train caught fresh horses out of the remuda, and they spurred onto the prairie in a lope, out across a bald hill and down the other side out of sight. There was no way anyone who was half watching could have missed them.

Isaac and Pete Runyan, making a point of not looking at each other, fell in behind the herd, putting in the appearance of making a hand while they waited for darkness.

Chapter Twelve

They had not told anyone what they were doing, but it appeared everyone guessed. When they reached Wash's camped wagon and the wrangler brought the remuda up so the men could catch their night horses, Runyan roped his own black. Hunter Proffitt said, "Isaac, I was thinkin' you ought to take that big dun of Joe Sample's. Joe won't need him for a while, and that dun'll carry you to hell and back."

Isaac took his advice. He thought Hunter had a right to resent the fact that the Major was sending Isaac and a near-stranger on this mission instead of himself. If such a resentment existed, it didn't show. Isaac wondered if Hunter sensed danger in it, and was simply glad he wasn't going.

I wisht I wasn't either, he thought.

He saddled the dun, having to let out his latigo a little because this horse was larger than the ones he had been accustomed to riding. The saddlebags weren't all that heavy, but imagination made them add a hundred pounds to the weight of the saddle. A tingle ran up and down his spine every time he touched them. He could not have been more nervous if he had carried three rattlesnakes in each bag.

I sure wouldn't be no happy rich man, he thought, *if money always made me this uneasy.*

Pete Runyan seemed to sense Isaac's feelings, and he came near smiling. "Want me to carry them for you?"

"We each got our orders," Isaac said stiffly.

They tied their horses as near the chuckwagon as custom allowed. Isaac made it a point to put the dun where he could easily watch it. He knew no one in this camp would consider taking that money, but the responsibility weighed heavily on him, nevertheless.

If I sweat like this all the way to Fort Worth, there won't be a hundred pounds left of me.

Isaac ordinarily stood back and let everybody else through the line first when supper was ready. This time he sensed that everybody was waiting for him and Pete Runyan. Runyan accepted their deference without hesitation. Isaac held back until Hunter Proffitt motioned with his chin. Then he took his plate and utensils and visited the pots and Dutch ovens.

Pete Runyan said, "You better eat aplenty. Pickin's may be thin from here on."

"You just watch out for yourownself," Isaac told him. He made his way to his place on the wagontongue. He had no appetite for the food, but he knew Pete Runyan was right; he had to eat whether he wanted to or not.

Wash worked his way around to him directly, glancing about to see if anyone could hear him. Accusingly he said, "I heard you sassin' that Mister Runyan. I swear, Isaac, you're goin' to get yourself hurt."

Wash was at it again, Isaac thought sourly.

Wash said, "Where you're goin', you might need that man almighty bad. You got no call to be antagonizin' him. Dammit, Isaac, you got to learn to bend a little."

"I'll bend," Isaac said, "and let him kiss my left hind cheek."

Wash shook his head in disgust. "I doubt as ever I'll see you alive again. If robbers don't kill you, Pete Runyan probably will."

"He'll have to work at it; I won't be just a-standin' there."

The sun was down, but it lacked some while being dark. Isaac stretched out on the ground where he could take a little rest, but where the dun horse was not out of his sight. He glanced over toward Pete Runyan's bedroll and thought the cowboy was probably lying asleep atop his blankets. That, Isaac thought, took a steadier nerve than *he* had. His skin was prickling with impatience to be up and riding.

When the sky was black and the stars were beginning to shine, Hunter Proffitt came around. "You-all ready?"

Wash brought two sacks, handing the first to Pete Runyan, the next to Isaac. "Some biscuits, some fried meat. Ain't much but you may not find no better. When a man's hungry enough, an old bullfrog tastes like chicken."

To Isaac's surprise, Pete Runyan smiled at the cook. "Wash, if you was lighter complected . . . and younger . . . and a woman, I believe I'd marry you."

Hunter Proffitt mounted his horse as Isaac and Runyan did. "I'll ride with you-all as far as the herd."

They moved away from the wagon in a trot, Isaac checking the saddlebags to be sure they were firmly tied and wouldn't work loose as a result of the jostling. The sack of food hung to one side and threw the load a little off-balance. He had originally planned to bring no blankets, for he doubted he would have much time to use them anyway. But he decided one rolled blanket tied behind the cantle would help keep the bulging saddlebags from being so conspicuous.

Chalk Denson was riding slowly on the near side of the herd. He halted as the three riders came up to him. He took a quick look at Isaac and Runyan. "Fixin' to go, are you?" he asked needlessly. When the two nodded, he said, "You better be a-lookin' sharp."

Runyan asked him why.

" 'Cause there's somebody out yonder."

Hunter Proffitt said, "You've seen somebody?"

"No, ain't seen nothin'."

"You've heard somebody?"

"Ain't heard them either. But I've felt them. I tell you, boys, I know there's somebody out there."

Proffitt studied him a long moment, doubting. "Coyotes, maybe. This is a hell of a country for coyotes."

Denson shook his head. "The *two*-legged kind."

Proffitt said, "It ain't likely. They'd of followed after Alf and the Major."

Denson replied, "Coyotes have got crafty ways, whether they're the four-legged kind or the other."

Proffitt turned to Pete Runyan. "Well, Pete, you can

take that for what it's worth. I expect he's just nervous, but it won't hurt if you watch yourselves. You got this ranch and our jobs packed in them saddlebags."

Runyan said, "You get these steers to the railroad, and we'll get the money to Fort Worth."

Proffitt nodded. "Have a couple of good drinks for us while you're there; it'll be a time before *we* have any."

Isaac and Runyan moved away from the herd in a trot to avoid startling the cattle. Once well clear, they swung into an easy lope. Isaac set the direction.

Runyan demanded, "You sure you're goin' the right way? Seems to me like Fort Worth ought to be a little more to the south."

"You ever been there?"

"Nope."

"Well, *I* been there lots of times. We got to make the OL Ranch to get us a change of horses tomorrow. The OL is thisaway."

"You get us lost and I just may skin you a little."

"Don't you worry about that; you just worry about keepin' up. I ain't waitin' for you if you fall behind."

They rode in the lope awhile, then let the horses drop down to a trot. When the horses seemed to have recovered their wind, Isaac would touch spurs to the big dun, putting him back into a lope. He had never ridden Joe Sample's horse before, but he had watched him under Joe and had always figured this horse could carry a rider about as long as the rider could hold up to it. He didn't know so much about Runyan's black, but he decided it was up to Runyan to know how much the horse could take.

He would not have told Runyan for a hundred dollars, but he was guessing to some degree just where the OL headquarters would be. He had been there with the Major on every trip they had made to Fort Worth, but they had always ridden in the daytime. He took a general reading on the stars and trusted the rest to instinct. When daylight came, perhaps there would be some familiar landmarks on which he could adjust. With any luck, he could manage it in such a gradual way that Runyan would never know.

They had been riding for perhaps half an hour when

Runyan held up his hand and pulled to a sudden halt. Isaac did likewise, puzzled. Runyan dismounted and turned his left ear to the direction from which they had come.

Isaac's saddle squeaked a little, so he stepped down too and listened. He heard nothing. He asked, "What did you hear, Runyan?"

Runyan did not answer him for a minute, still listening hard. Finally he shook his head. "Not a damned thing. But I got to studyin' what Chalk Denson said. I thought if there was somebody back there, maybe we could hear them."

All Isaac heard was the gentle wind in his ear and the soft rub of leather as the saddles gave and took to the horses' breathing.

Runyan shrugged. "Chalk Denson always struck me as bein' somethin' of an old woman anyway. Let's go."

They remounted and took Isaac's direction again, loping. The horses could have run much faster if they had to, but they could not have held it up long. This alternating of a lope and a trot could cover a lot of miles before the horses finally gave out. It pleased Isaac to be the one who set the pace, who indicated when they speeded up and when they slowed down. It gave him a measure of power over Pete Runyan, modest though it might be.

Stars changed position through the night, which was one way a cowboy had of telling time. For that reason Isaac did not try to pick one star and ride to it. Instead, he positioned himself so that his left shoulder was pointed almost at the north star; that was one star which always stayed the same. He rode for hours without saying a word, except once when the dun stumbled and almost went down in a prairie dog hole. Even then he spoke to the horse rather than to Runyan. When dawn began to break in the east, he knew they had put a lot of miles behind them. They had pushed these horses as hard as Isaac had dared, and if they didn't make the OL by the middle of the morning they were going to find themselves moving in a walk.

Dawn showed him what he had hoped, a string of hills to the northwest. He recognized a stand of cottonwoods as being at a spring on the west part of the OL; he and the Major had watered their horses there on every trip. Isaac pulled a little to the left to make the cotton-woods.

"Water," he said, pointing.

Runyan replied crisply, "You can still talk; I thought you'd bitten your tongue off."

"I didn't see where we had anything to talk about."

"I reckon we don't. But it gets a little spooky to ride along with a ghost all night."

"I thought all ghosts was white."

"So did I."

Inwardly, Isaac smiled, liking the idea of getting under Runyan's hide. He dismounted at the spring and loosened the cinch. The horses drank gratefully. Runyan moved as near the spring's bubbling flow as he could and began to drink.

Wantin' to get it ahead of me, Isaac thought, more resigned than resentful. *Afraid I'll poison him if he drinks after me.*

Finished, Runyan wiped his sleeve across his mouth. "How far now to where we get a change of horses?"

"A ways."

That didn't tell Runyan much, but Isaac didn't *intend* to. Isaac had been brought up to do lots of looking and ask no needless questions. He had no great patience with anyone who did not follow the same code.

Runyan said, "Then we ought to eat a little somethin' while we let these horses stand and blow." He dug into his sack and brought out some cold meat and a couple of Wash's big biscuits.

Isaac knew that was a good idea, so he did likewise, then stretched out on the ground for a few minutes of rest before they continued their journey. He found himself looking surreptitiously at Pete Runyan. Isaac felt the beginnings of fatigue and thought he could see the same in Runyan. But the cowboy wasn't saying anything about it, and Isaac guessed he wouldn't. Whatever other short-comings Runyan might have, he wasn't weak, and he was not a complainer.

Well, if they were tired now, they'd be a lot worse off before they were through. Nearest Isaac could guess, they would have to ride all day today, all night, and a good part of tomorrow to get to Fort Worth. Any rest they got would come in small dabs.

There wasn't much grass around the spring; cattle kept it grazed off that near to water. The horses started nosing around for something to eat, so Isaac decided it was time to be moving on. The horses would have lots of time for grazing when they were unsaddled and turned loose. Without saying anything, Isaac pushed to his feet and started tightening his cinch.

Runyan did the same, saying, "I was wonderin' when you'd decide you'd rested your lazy butt long enough."

"I was just thinkin' of you," Isaac told him, swinging up and starting off, letting Runyan push to catch up with him.

With daylight, Isaac looked back a couple of times to see if anyone was coming along on their backtrail. He thought once he saw somebody, but on a harder look he decided it was three loose horses, way back a mile or more. In this open ranch country, horses grazed wherever they took the notion.

It was past midmorning when the OL headquarters layout appeared ahead of them, and another hour before they reached it. Isaac noted with satisfaction that dust was rising from the corrals. Maybe they wouldn't have to hunt Ollie Leindecker down.

Isaac could always tell when a horse was tiring beneath him, and he knew the dun was rapidly running out his string. He guessed by looking that Runyan's black was the same. The two men rode across a narrow stream that flowed out of a spring downhill from the small frame house Leindecker had built for his family. Through the dust Isaac could tell that cowboys were riding broncs. He could hear the men's good-natured shouting, and the snorting and wind-breaking of the horses as they pitched around in a circular corral.

Just seeing it made him feel more tired even than he was. But it also brought back to him the memory of the day he had bested Pete Runyan on the bay bronc. That memory always roused a little glow in Isaac.

Ollie Leindecker wasn't riding any broncs himself; that was what he hired someone else for. But he was helping with the rope work when he saw the two riders. He handed the rope to somebody and moved to the fence, trying to see clearer through the haze of dust.

"It's me, Mister Leindecker," Isaac said. "Isaac Jefford."

Leindecker blinked eyes that watered from the biting dust. It was hard to tell what color his thick moustache was supposed to be, for it was powdered with dirt. "Sure," he said, "I know you. Where's the Major at?"

"He sent us on an errand for him. Said to see if you'd lend us a couple of fresh horses. It's all here in this letter."

Isaac fished from his shirt pocket a letter the Major had given him to show to Leindecker and other ranchers en route. He had also authorized Isaac and Runyan to take a little money out of the bags, if necessary, to buy or rent horses in case they could not find any to borrow.

Leindecker gave the letter only a moment's quick glance. "If the Major says you need it, and I got it, you can have it." He motioned for them to follow him. He led them afoot to another pen a little way from the bronc corral. "Some good usin' horses in here," he said, pointing. "Whichaway you boys headed?"

"We got to make Fort Worth by sometime tomorrow," Isaac told him.

Leindecker shook his head. "You can't do it. Even if you ride till dark and start at daylight, you can't do it."

Runyan said, "We figured on ridin' all night."

Leindecker stared hard at first one, then the other. "You didn't sleep last night either, did you?"

Runyan said they hadn't.

Leindecker frowned. "You must need to get there almighty bad."

Isaac agreed. "Almighty bad."

Leindecker took a rope from a saddle on a rack and walked out toward a dozen or so horses in the big pen. "That bein' the case, I'll give you the best I got." He swung a quick figure-eight loop and led out a blue roan for Runyan. He glanced at Isaac's saddle as it slid down from the dun. "Them saddlebags look awful fat."

Isaac knew he was guessing close. He didn't figure it

would hurt for Leindecker to know. "They'll thin up when we get to Fort Worth."

Leindecker caught him another dun, a little less thick in the chest but longer of leg than the one he had been riding. "He can run like hell if you need him to," Leindecker said.

Isaac replied, "I hope we don't need him to. But if somebody was to come along and ask about us, it wouldn't hurt if you could lie a little bit. Might save this horse a run."

Leindecker chuckled dryly. "If I got any talent in this world besides tradin' horses, it's tellin' lies. Come to think of it, that's one and the same."

Isaac saddled quickly, for Runyan already had a little lead on him. "I sure do appreciate the borry of the horses, Mister Leindecker."

"Bring me a bottle of good Fort Worth whiskey when you come back, if you can manage it. Otherwise, it's all free."

"We'll do it," Isaac promised as his rump hit the saddle. He spurred out to catch up with Runyan, who already was fifty yards ahead of him.

Before long Isaac was wishing they had hit the OL ranch at dinnertime; even a cup of strong black coffee alone would have helped. But they would have wasted an hour if they had waited around for dinner; maybe two by the time they ate and got away. He doubted they could afford two hours. He dug into his sack and took the edge off his hunger by eating a biscuit and a piece of cold beef.

Runyan gave him a quick glance. "Weakenin' are you, boy?"

"Just takin' nourishment. I'll still be goin' when you're laid out on your back."

The noonday heat built, not peaking until far along in the afternoon. Isaac pushed the horses harder now, knowing they should reach the Coker place before dark; there they ought to be able to change again. He looked back occasionally, never quite satisfied. At no time did he see anything that looked threatening, yet at no time could he see far enough or clearly enough to be absolutely sure no one was moving along their backtrail, far enough behind them not to show plainly through the dancing heatwaves.

Several hours passed without a word between the two men. At length Runyan said, "I believe Leindecker gave you the best of the deal. This roan of mine is playin' out."

"Maybe it's the way you sit your saddle," Isaac said, knowing it wasn't true but unable to resist taking a small dig at the cowboy. "Some people just naturally wear a horse down more than others do."

The Coker ranch looked like a poverty spread, but it had a better foundation than appearances would indicate. Old Man Coker simply did not spend money for anything that did not mean more or better cattle and horses, or more and better range for them. A fancy house did not help the grass grow or mean a bigger calf crop. He still lived in a picket house made of live-oak trunks, plastered with mud to keep the rain and wind out.

The Major's note did not mean as much to the brown-bearded Coker as it had to Leindecker. His calculating eyes appraised the tired horses Isaac and Runyan rode. "I ain't sure I got any horses to spare, especially if you aim to ride mine like *them* has been rode. Break a man's horses down, you'd just as well shoot them."

Isaac said, "Major Lytton will pay you any damages you feel like you got comin'."

Coker's eyes narrowed. He cast a hard glance at Runyan. "What's the matter with *you*? You let a black boy do all your talkin' for you?"

"He's talkin' pretty good," Runyan said flatly. "If *he* don't get what we come for, then *I'll* start. I think you'd rather listen to *him*."

The threat was there, and Coker did not miss it. "Seein' as it's the Major, and he's got a reputation for bein' a fair man, you can have the horses. But I want it understood that if they come up drawed or lame or anything the Major's goin' to owe me."

Isaac said, "Understood."

Coker looked at Runyan. "I'll want *your* word on that."

Runyan said impatiently, "Isaac has got authority to speak for the Major."

Coker evidently had a good eye for horses, because he didn't catch any of his better ones. He picked a bay for Runyan and then roped out a black for Isaac. "This one ought to fit *you*," he said.

As they rode away, Runyan was grumbling about the bay's rough trot. "Fine friends *you* got."

"He wasn't no friend of *mine*."

"That is the damned truth. I bet supper was about ready at the house, but he didn't invite us up to eat with him."

You wouldn't of eaten with me if he had, Isaac thought.

He looked back at the squat, unpretty spread of the Coker place. "Runyan, I see some men on horseback ridin' up to the corrals."

Runyan stopped and looked back. "Cowboys, more than likely. Workin' for that damned Coker, poor bastards."

"You *sure* they're cowboys?"

"I ain't sure of nothin' except I wisht I had quit workin' for this outfit two weeks ago. Let's whip up a little."

They pushed the horses hard for a while, making some distance. But there came a time when they had to slow up for the horses' sake. Isaac didn't figure they would have a chance to change before sometime tomorrow morning; these horses had to carry them all night. He looked back, but he could no longer see the ranch headquarters. They had put a couple of hills behind them, and a brushy draw.

"Probably just cowboys, is all it was," Runyan said.

Isaac frowned. "One thing about it, if it's *not* cowboys . . . if it's somebody followin' after us . . . they're as tired as we are."

"Well," said Runyan, "let's not give them no time to rest."

Chapter Thirteen

They pushed into the night, alternating between a lope and a good solid mile-eating trot as they had done from the start. The lack of sleep weighed heavily on Isaac now, and he knew it must be doing the same to Runyan. It was a point of pride with Isaac not to say a word about it. When he figured back, he knew he hadn't really slept in upwards of forty hours. It was sometimes said of a cow outfit that the hands had more need for a lantern than for a bed, but this was stretching endurance toward the breaking point.

So long as they were in a lope, Isaac was all right; the harder pace kept him awake. But when they slowed to a trot he would begin nodding off to uneasy sleep, instinct holding him in the saddle. Most cowboys developed the knack of sleeping while they rode; now and then that ability served them well.

Runyan's voice brought Isaac suddenly awake, surprising him so that he lost balance and slid to one side, catching himself by grabbing the saddlehorn.

"You're asleep," Runyan accused him.

Isaac knew he was, but he would not admit it to Runyan. "I'm awake. I been awake all along."

Runyan stopped his horse. "Like hell. But if you won't unbend a little, I'll do it. I'll call the halt."

Isaac protested, "We can't afford to stop."

"We can't afford *not* to. You're asleep in the saddle, and I'm not far from it. An hour of rest might be the difference between us gettin' there and not makin' it atall."

Isaac knew it was a good idea, but he couldn't accept it from this self-appointed paragon. "You stop now and I'll ride off and leave you."

"How far do you think you'd get? You'd fall out of that saddle in half a mile. There's a little stand of post oaks here where we can tie the horses." Runyan dismounted. "Get down, Isaac."

"You tryin' to be boss now?"

"I'm tellin' you to get down."

"The Major said *I* was the boss over the travelin' part. You're only the boss if we get in trouble."

"The Major ain't nowhere around. Anyway, I figure we're in trouble. You goin' to get off of that horse, or am I goin' to pull you off?"

Isaac braced his hands against his saddlehorn. "They freed all the slaves, or have you forgot?"

"I'm fixin' to forget you're the Major's pet and fetch you a hard clout right between the eyes."

"You better not try it, you white trash. . . ."

Runyan moved so quickly Isaac barely saw his hands reach up. Rough hands grabbed at Isaac's shirt. Before he could try to wrestle them loose, Runyan gave him a violent jerk. Isaac tumbled out of the saddle, landing hard on his sore side.

Runyan gritted, "Now, damn you, you'll move when I tell you."

Isaac's horse shied at the sudden movement, and Runyan grabbed the reins to keep it from running away. That gave Isaac time to catch a quick breath before he pushed to his feet. As he came up, his right fist was swinging. Pete Runyan's head jerked at the impact. Runyan stumbled and fell on his back, both feet going up in the air, the spurs jingling.

Isaac caught the reins that Runyan had so suddenly lost and started to lead both horses to the post oaks. Runyan got up onto one knee, and as he did his right hand came up with the pistol from his hip. Isaac swallowed hard, looking down the barrel. He raised his eyes a little, and even in the moonlight he could see rage in Runyan's face. Isaac stiffened, expecting Runyan to pull the trigger. Cold sweat broke.

Runyan held the pistol on him a long moment. Finally he said, "If I knew the way to Fort Worth, I believe by God I'd shoot you!"

Isaac had no answer to that, and his mouth was too dry even if he had known what to say.

Runyan lowered the pistol, and Isaac knew he would not shoot . . . at least not now.

Runyan said, "Tie your horse, Isaac." Runyan grabbed his own reins. Isaac led his mount to the nearest post oak tree, loosened the cinch, and tied a half hitch in the leather lines.

He turned then to see Runyan, but all he saw was that fist, a split second before it hit him squarely across the nose. Isaac fell back against his horse. He thought the animal would break the reins. Isaac moved away from it, edging sideways so that his eyes never left Runyan. Runyan kept pressing in closer, and when Isaac thought the distance was right he took a step forward, his right fist swinging with all the strength that was in him. He staggered Runyan.

Runyan stood there feeling his face; Isaac could see it was bleeding a little. He caught the salty taste of blood from his own lip.

Runyan muttered, "White trash, eh? Boy, that's one thing you oughtn't to've called me."

He came trudging back, fist driving. Isaac saw it this time and knew he could not dodge it, so he moved forward and caught it halfway, countering with a blow of his own. Runyan's fist hurt him, badly, but maybe Runyan was being hurt too.

Runyan went down on one knee, tried to rise but couldn't. Breathing hard, Isaac stood over him, fists still clenched, his arms up protectively.

The words came with difficulty. "I called you white trash . . . because that's all you are. . . . Come onto the ranch . . . put on all them airs . . . better'n anybody. . . . But you ain't better'n *me* . . . I proved that. To me you're just . . . white trash."

Runyan gave a cry of anger and rushed him, throwing Isaac backward. Isaac lost most of what breath he had left. Runyan was on top of him a minute, hitting him with his fist, but that fist no longer had any strength behind it. Isaac gave a lunge to one side, throwing Runyan down. Runyan groped for something to grab to, to pull himself up, but Isaac climbed astraddle of him. However, he found that now, like Runyan, he had no strength. The blows he delivered were weak. Runyan got his arms around Isaac's body and wrestled free. They faced each other on their knees, gasping for air, hopelessly pounding each other with fists they could barely lift, fists that carried no injury.

Before long it was all either could do to stay up on hands and knees, still facing but no longer able even to take a swing. Runyan wheezed like a horse choking on a rope, and Isaac felt sharp pain lance through his bruised left side with every breath he drew.

Runyan dropped and lay on his stomach, still making a harsh sound in his throat as he struggled for air. Isaac let himself go to the ground and rolled over on his back, hoping to take some of the pressure off his aching side. His dry throat burned as if he had been breathing flame. He wanted to think he had won the fight, but he knew it was no more than a standoff. If anything, both had lost it.

It was awhile before Isaac's breathing was normal enough and his throat wet enough that he could speak. Stubbornly he gasped, "Just the same . . . I still say you're white trash."

Runyan made an effort to answer, but nothing came. He lay awhile in silence, except for his labored breathing. At length he cleared his throat and spat a few times. He felt his face and evidently satisfied himself that his nose wasn't broken. Then he lay on his stomach awhile longer, head propped on his arms, his eyes on Isaac.

Finally he said, "Been a many a year since anybody's called me what you did."

Isaac by now was beginning to wish he hadn't, but he wouldn't give Runyan the satisfaction of his saying so.

Runyan said, "Bein' a slave like you was, I don't reckon you ever knew your daddy."

"Sure I knew my daddy. Why wouldn't I?"

"The way they traded slaves around, and all. . . ."

"My daddy was still with us when freedom come. I knew him."

Runyan said bitterly, "I wisht I hadn't known *mine*
. . . worthless old reprobate."

Isaac raised up on one skinned elbow, a little scandalized. "You'd talk thataway about your own daddy?"

"It's true. He was a whiskey-drinkin' old soak, never
had more than six bits at one time in all those years.
Drug us around with him till he got tired of it, then went
off and left us. White trash, they called us, on account of
him."

"But he was still your daddy."

"White trash. People looked down on us worse than
they looked down on their niggers. When I was a kid I
had to work in the fields alongside them rich folks'
slaves. They paid us next to nothin' and worked us like
dogs. If they had a job a little dangerous or apt to hurt
somebody, they wouldn't let them lazy pets of theirs do
it; *they* was worth money. They'd make *us* do it because
we was just no-account white trash. Them lazy pet
darkys'd lay off on us every time they could, and leave
the heavy stuff to us."

His voice was caustic. "I swore it wouldn't always
be thataway. I swore someday I'd be the best at anything
and everything I ever done, and by God I am! Been a long
time since anybody's called me white trash. If *you* ever
do it again, I swear I'll shoot you right between the
eyes!"

Runyan fell silent, and Isaac knew he had soon
dropped into the fitful sleep of exhaustion. Isaac rubbed
his hand across his battered face a couple of times, and
he was gone too.

He didn't know how long he had slept, but a sound
brought him suddenly awake. He raised up, all senses
alert. He turned his head slowly, listening. He heard it
again . . . hoofbeats.

He took two long steps to Runyan and gently shook
his shoulder, then clapped his hand over Runyan's mouth
as the cowboy awoke with a start. Isaac pointed in the
direction of the sound. He still could not see far into the
night, but he saw the tied horses' ears prick forward.
Horses could see better at night than men could, and they
had an ear for the sound of other horses. Quickly Isaac
walked over and covered the black horse's nose with his

hand to prevent him from nickering. Runyan lost no time in doing the same with his bay.

Isaac thought at first that what he heard might be loose horses. But then came a faint jingle, keeping time to the rhythm of a horse's movements. Spur rowels, or perhaps a curb chain.

Gradually he could make out the shapes in the night. Three horses, three riders, skirting around the post oak motte. Isaac watched, his mouth sagging open as he contemplated the portent of this.

Pete Runyan whispered in disgust. "Goddamn them, don't they ever sleep?"

Isaac made no answer until the men were well past. He said, "Chalk Denson was right. They been there all along."

"Doggin' our trail, stayin' far enough back not to come up on us till they was ready. They probably figured we'd ride all night. Us stoppin' to rest throwed them a little."

"They won't stay throwed. They know whichaway Fort Worth is, same as we do."

"Probably figured on takin' us in the mornin', catchin' us too tired and wore out to be keepin' a watchful eye."

Isaac hurriedly tightened his cinch, any thought of sleep lost in a burst of nervous energy. "All of a sudden I ain't nowhere near as tired as I was."

"There's more than one way to get to Fort Worth, I'd think. If they're goin' *that* way, then let's me and you go *this* way." Runyan made a sign with his hand indicating a wide swing around.

Isaac didn't figure he had to say anything; the need was obvious. "What worries me is the Major. What do you reckon they done with the Major?"

"*Nothin'*, is my guess. I'll bet they never took after the Major in the first place. I'll bet they smelled a nigger in the woodpile."

"Meanin' me?"

"You generally go with the Major when he makes a money trip to Fort Worth, don't you?"

"Usually."

"The man that shot at you—that Quain—he knew it, didn't he?"

"He wasn't on the ranch all that long, but he probably heard talk around the wagon."

"Well, this time you didn't go with the Major. Maybe this Quain's nose got to twitchin', and he figured it out."

"I never taken him to be that smart."

"Nothin' like the smell of money to sharpen a man's wits. It was only our good luck that let them run past us. I say when you got a streak of good luck, play it. Let's get ridin'." Runyan gasped and grabbed at his side as he started to climb into the saddle. Isaac figured he had gotten a couple of good licks in on him before his strength gave out. Runyan caught him looking and quickly dropped his hand away, hiding the pain. He said, "You'll remember that stoppin' was *my* idea. Turned out a good thing we done it."

Isaac didn't figure he had any call to reply. He mounted, hoping the three men were past hearing distance. He and Runyan held the horses to a trot awhile, for the sound of a trotting horse does not carry as far as the drumming of a lope. They swung to the north and east, putting two or three hills between themselves and the three men.

There was no longer any thought of sleep. The hour or so they had rested, plus the excitement of discovery, had given Isaac strength he did not know he had. It had done the same for Runyan, he judged.

They were many miles to the northward when dawn came, riding on a course roughly parallel to the one they would have followed had they not discovered pursuit. Anxiety prickled Isaac's skin as daylight broke across the open, grassy, rolling hills. It would not take the three long now to discover that they had lost their quarry, that they were no longer on the right trail.

That anxiety made him press these horses harder than he had pushed the others before them. He kept them in a lope longer at a time, until at last he could not ignore the fact that they were giving out. He was not on familiar ground now. He knew the general lay of the land, but he did not know the whereabouts of the various ranches and their headquarters.

Runyan seemed to read his thoughts. "You lost, boy?"

"I know where Fort Worth is at, but I don't know where to go to find us a change of horses. We're fixin' to need them mighty bad."

"Your friend Coker didn't do us no favors."

"He's no friend of mine."

"Nor of anybody else's." Oddly then, Runyan chuckled.

Irritated, Isaac said, "I don't know what you see to laugh at."

"It just come to me that them three boys probably got fresh horses from Coker too. I'll bet they wasn't as nice to him as we was. I hope they set fire to the old whelp's beard."

"They'll try to set fire to *us* if they catch up to us."

From far behind them Isaac heard a shot. Instinctively he ducked. Then he heard two more shots in quick succession and knew them for what they were: a signal.

Runyan had quit chuckling. "They fanned out at daylight to hunt for our tracks. One of them has found what he was lookin' for."

"That was a stupid thing for them to do, fire them shots. If we hadn't already known they was after us, we'd know it now."

"No matter. They probably figure it's a horserace from here on anyway. They got from here to Fort Worth to catch up with us."

Isaac spurred the black horse but felt little response; the animal was nearing its limit. "I hope Coker gave them fellers a worse deal on horses than he gave us."

"More likely they just went in there and took what they wanted. We better find us a remount or the sweet-milk is fixin' to clabber on us."

They had ridden for another half hour, getting no more than a good trot from the horses, when they saw a house and barns and corrals set on a slope toward the bottom of a long, high hill. Isaac and Runyan glanced at each other and without a word pointed their horses in that direction. First one then the other would look back every few minutes. They still had not seen anyone, but that was of little comfort.

This place was strange to Isaac; he and the Major had never come by here on their trips to Fort Worth. The house was a small frame structure, set up two feet high on heavy oak posts. Three dogs lay in the shade beneath the house until the horsemen approached the main corral gate; then they came bounding out barking and raising cain. By the barn, Isaac saw a pen with four horses in it. A man stepped to the door of a small shed that Isaac took to be a blacksmith shop. He was hatless, had his sleeves rolled up, and was carrying a big hammer. His old shirt was soaked with sweat.

"How do, fellers?" he said as Isaac and Runyan swung wearily from their saddles.

"Not so good," Runyan told him. "We need to borry two horses from you."

Any friendliness quickly disappeared. The man critically studied the two riders' battered faces and evidently did not care for what he saw. "You fellers have had a tangle with somebody," he said suspiciously. "Your faces are still bloody. You in some kind of trouble?"

Isaac handed him the Major's letter. The man scanned it, shaking his head. "I don't know no Major Lytton."

Isaac said, "We'll *buy* two horses from you if we have to. But we got to have them, and have them right now."

The man's eyes hardened. "What kind of trouble are you in?"

"We got to get to Fort Worth and do it in a hurry. There's some men comin' back yonder that don't intend for us to get there. We *got* to have fresh horses."

The man raised the hammer as if to get it into position to swing. "A posse, more than likely. Be damned if I'm goin' to help somebody get away from a posse. You-all get on your horses and be gone from here, right now!"

Isaac decided he had to tell him all of it. "We're carryin' money. Them other fellers are robbers."

The man's suspicions only deepened. "Money? Where would the likes of you get money? One black

. . . one ragged-shirt cowpuncher . . . if you got any money you stole it. That's why they're after you. Now I'll tell you one more time . . . *git!*" He raised the hammer a little higher.

Isaac was inclined to argue further, but Runyan broke in. "Step back, Isaac, you done your part. Now we're down to what *I* come for." He slipped the saddlegun out of its scabbard and brought it to bear on the man. "Now, Mister, you just drop that hammer like it was a red-hot horseshoe or I'll put a swallow fork in your left ear!"

The man's mouth went open, but he held onto the hammer. Runyan fired a shot that plowed through the wall and sent splinters flying. The man dropped the hammer.

A hard grin broke across Runyan's face as he glanced at Isaac. "See there, black boy? All it takes is the knowin' how. Now you peel them saddles off and go catch us two horses out of that pen."

Isaac did the job in a hurry while Runyan held the rifle on the rancher. He heard Runyan asking if the man's name might happen to be Coker. When the man said it wasn't, Runyan said, "We met a man named Coker last night. Thought you two might be brothers."

Isaac saddled the two horses. Runyan asked the rancher, "What do you figure these two are worth?" The man told him one had cost him sixty-five dollars, the other eighty. Runyan said, "Isaac, give him two hundred dollars. That's to show we ain't horsethieves. If things work out, we'll be around and sell them back to you for fifty dollars apiece. That'll allow you a hundred profit for wear and tear."

He jerked his head toward the gate. "Let all them other horses out, Isaac. We'll run them off a ways so them fellers back yonder won't find no remount here."

Isaac ran the horses out of the pen. Runyan told the rancher, "If I was you, I'd take me a nice long walk down the draw for a while. There's three old boys behind us that'll be droppin in on you directly, and they may not be as sociable as we was. Let's go, Isaac."

They struck a lope due into the morning sun that had already climbed well up in a cloudless sky. They put a couple of miles behind them before they came into a brushy draw. Runyan chased the loose horses into it and then slowed down. "I hope the boys will overlook them."

Isaac said, "That feller had a right to be suspicious of us, the way we looked. You was pretty rough on him."

"We got the horses; that's the main thing. How far you figure it is now to Fort Worth?"

"Can't tell for sure; we're off the trail the Major and I always taken. I'd guess we ought to get there this afternoon."

"If we don't get there while the bank's still open, it's all for nothin'."

"We'll get there," Isaac said grimly, spurring back into a lope.

But presently he knew he had to slow down. Fresh horses wouldn't stay fresh long if they punished them this way. Regretfully he pulled his bay horse down to a trot.

This was a different kind of country than he knew out west. It was made up of tall, rounded hills, the grass standing belly-high to a horse, and every hill looked about the same as every other. Each time he climbed one he hoped to see Fort Worth on the other side. But as he topped over, all he could see was more hills.

Runyan said, "You'd think if we was all that close to town we'd run into a good wagon road by and by."

"We're all right," Isaac said. "The direction is good; it's just the distance I ain't sure about."

Climbing these hills was hard on the horses, and he went around as many as he could, though this took a little more time and had the effect of putting them off-course now and again. He hoped he wasn't wasting too much traveling.

The sun reached its high point almost directly over-head. Weariness weighed heavily on Isaac again, and he found his vision blurring sometimes. Brief periods of excitement such as hearing the three shots this morning and the encounter with the rancher had given him an artificial stimulus at the time, but that had long since worn off. Once as they trotted along he caught himself almost slipping out of the saddle, more asleep than awake. He rubbed his eyes and wished for a good drink of cool water, anything to bring him wide awake again.

He fished in the food sack but found the meat beginning to smell, either from spoilage or from horsesweat. Either way, he couldn't eat it. He let the sack drop to the ground. He plodded along fighting against sleep and losing the battle.

Runyan's voice broke through to him, and he jerked erect, startled. "Isaac, you awake?"

Blinking, Isaac said, "Sure, I ain't been asleep."

"You'll wake up now. They've caught up to us."

Isaac turned in the saddle, searching desperately. "Where?"

Runyan slipped his saddlegun out of its scabbard, pointing to the south and east. "There."

Isaac saw the three men spurring their horses, circling around in an effort to get ahead of him and Runyan. He saw what they were heading for, a little motte of trees at the bottom of a hill. It was the only cover in sight. Drawing his own carbine he said, "If they ever get in there they can shoot at us in the wide open, and there's not a Chinaman's chance *we* can hit one of *them*."

"Then," Runyan said, "let's beat them to it."

They jabbed spurs into their horses' ribs and went into a hard run, cutting through that tall grass, shattering the matured seedheads and leaving them floating in the wind. Runyan used his quirt, lashing his horse's rump on the right side, then swinging it around in front of him and reaching back to hit him on the left. The speed and the warm wind stung Isaac's sleepless eyes. He kept the spurs working.

On the right flank he could see the three horsemen in a blur, coming at an oblique angle, all five men converging on the motte. For a minute or two it looked to Isaac as if the race was nip and tuck. Then he knew that he and Runyan were in the lead; the robbers had not found fresh horses.

"Keep a-spurrin' him, Isaac," Runyan shouted. "We ain't got far to go."

The three robbers saw how the race was going, and they drove their mounts for all the speed they could get. But now it became apparent they were going to lose.

Isaac saw one of them begin reining up, pulling to a stop. "What the hell . . ."

The man swung out of the saddle, a rifle in his hand. "Look out, Runyan!" Isaac shouted, not knowing which of them was to be the target. He leaned way over his horse's neck. He saw a blossom of smoke from the saddlegun and heard a horse squeal. Where Runyan and his horse had been, Isaac saw a blur of brown hide and shod hoofs as the horse pitched headlong into the grass and rolled over. He saw Runyan slide clear, grabbing desperately at his fallen rifle. Isaac brought his bay horse around and started to circle back. Runyan, pushing up from his belly, waved him away. "Go on! Beat them to that motte or we're dead!"

He saw that Runyan was right. The time he would spend picking up the cowboy would allow the other two horsemen to get to the timber ahead of him. Then, under that cover, they could have themselves a shooting gallery.

He wickedly jabbed spurs to the bay hide and kept riding, bent low over the saddlehorn. He kicked his feet free of the stirrups, for if that rifleman got another good shot and hit this bay horse, Isaac didn't want to be pinned under it or hung to the saddle. He heard a shot and knew it was aimed at him; but he also knew that if he heard it, it had already missed.

Isaac reached the motte first and swung the bay horse around, firing two shots at the oncoming riders before he took time to get out of the saddle. Then, as he hit the ground he dropped to one knee, raised the saddlegun, and fired a third time. One of the horses fell as Runyan's had fallen, except that this one fell on its rider. Neither horse nor man got up.

The other horseman saw he was riding directly into the muzzle of a rifle. Desperately he reined his red roan around. In the moment that Isaac was levering a fresh cartridge into the chamber he recognized Alvin Quain. A surge of hatred came to him, and he brought the rifle up, trying to draw a fresh bead. But Quain was moving fast, and Isaac missed him.

A couple of bullets cut into the foilage around him. That first horseman, off out in the open, was firing at him.

Chapter Fourteen

Isaac's bay horse pulled back in fright, jerking at the reins. Isaac knew he could not hold the horse and fire that rifle with any accuracy. But if he let the horse go, it would run off and take the money with it. For a moment Isaac had to turn his back on the fire and do something about his horse. He shook down his rope, tied one end around the animal's neck with a firm knot that wouldn't slip and choke him, then tied a quick half hitch around a post oak stump.

He had a moment then to size up the situation. The fallen horse, fifty feet out from the thicket, still kicked a little in its death throes. The man pinned under it was not moving at all. Isaac realized the man's neck had been broken by the fall.

I killed him, he realized. *I shot the horse but I killed the man.* He had seen men die in the big war, but he had not personally killed anyone before. He guessed he would feel regretful about it later on, when he had time to worry about it. Right now he was too busy.

He looked for Runyan and had a hard time finding him. He could see Runyan's downed horse, but the cowboy was nowhere in sight. Then Isaac made out a movement in the tall grass, a movement that did not fit the easy back-and-forth seesawing of the grass in the wind. He made out a patch of color and knew Runyan was crawling toward the motte, letting the grass cover him from the remaining two horsemen.

Quain and his cohort were together now, both standing behind their horses two hundred yards away, probably counseling on what to do next. That they had

lost their first play for the money would not cause them
to give up. If Isaac had the advantage of the motte and its
cover, the other two had the advantage of free movement. Moreover, they had the advantage of time.

Well, Isaac thought, *one thing I can do is set them
afoot.* He rested the barrel of the rifle against a post oak
trunk and drew a careful bead on Quain's horse.
Through the smoke that curled away from his barrel he
saw he had missed. The wind was a factor. He could not
tell where the slug had gone . . . whether he had allowed too much windage or not enough. He tried another bead and squeezed the trigger. He saw Quain's
horse rear up and jerk the reins from Quain's hand. The
horse galloped away. Quain chased after it afoot but
only made the horse run faster.

Isaac frowned. Badly as he hated to, he had intended
to kill the horse. But making it run away served the same
purpose and saved the animal. It wouldn't quit traveling,
probably, until it returned to wherever it had come from.

Isaac looked regretfully at the other horse. He remembered stories he had heard about Indian fights. It
seemed the horses always caught more hell than the men
did; they were, after all, much better targets. Isaac had
never shot a horse except a couple of times out of abso-
lute necessity, in cases of injuries. It had been almost as
hard on him as if he had shot a child.

But he had it to do, and he leveled the rifle, drawing
a fresh bead. Before he could squeeze the trigger, he saw
the horse go down.

He raised his head up from the stock and stared,
puzzled. Then it came to him that Quain and the other
man had probably gotten a rope around the horse's feet
and had thrown it to protect it from Isaac's fire. He could
see a flurry of movement and guessed they were tying the
animal's feet to keep it down. This was the only horse
they had left; they had no intention of losing it.

It graveled Isaac to realize he probably wouldn't
have thought of that. But, he decided, a man who lives
like a coyote develops coyote ways.

Now he could see Runyan, closer but still crawling.
Bent low, Isaac started out from the motte to help him,

but Runyan waved him away. "Get back in there. You want them to kill you?"

Punctuating Runyan's command, a bullet clipped into the motte and sent cut leaves fluttering to the ground. Isaac could hear his horse back in there plunging and jerking futilely at the rope that held it. He pulled back into the cover and waited for Runyan.

He expected the cowboy to jump to his feet and sprint the last few feet, for the two outlaws could not have drawn a bead on him that fast. But Runyan kept crawling. For the first time Isaac realized the cowboy was hurt. Disregarding Runyan's protests, Isaac ran out to help him. A bullet cut harmlessly into the trees overhead as he dragged Runyan to cover.

Isaac's mouth was so dry he could hardly speak. "I didn't know you was shot."

"I ain't," Runyan said, his face twisted. "I broke my leg."

There was no question of it. Runyan's right leg was twisted in an unnatural shape below the knee. Isaac looked at it and breathed, "Jesus!"

Runyan tried to straighten himself out and lean against a tree. He cursed long and violently at the pain.

Isaac found himself sympathetic, which surprised him a little; for weeks now he had wished to see Runyan in just such a condition. "Hurts pretty bad, I'll bet."

"Hell yes, it hurts. But mostly I'm cussin' myself for gettin' into this kind of a mess in the first place. That Goddamned Major and his Goddamned bonus. I ought to've known when I rode off with you that I'd wind up in some kind of a jam."

Isaac's sympathy began to ebb. "Me? What did *I* do that got you a broken leg?"

Runyan had no answer; he just cursed some more. That leg must be giving him some agony. He said, "I wisht we had a little whiskey."

"We ain't even got any water," Isaac pointed out.

Runyan sat where he could look out across the grass at the two robbers' general position, though they were keeping their heads down, using the tall grass for cover. At length Runyan said, "As I was crawlin' up here, I had a lot of time to study the lay of the land. Seems to me like there's a low 'saddle' in the hills behind this motte. If a man was to have a little luck, he could bust out the back side of this motte and make it across that saddle before they could get a good clean bead on him."

Isaac hadn't had time to make that close a study. He walked back where the brush was thinner and took a look. Runyan was right. A rider would be in the open and exposed to fire for perhaps seventy-five yards. After that, he would be out of sight.

Isaac said, "You think you can ride the horse?"

"With this leg? Dammit, Isaac, you *are* dumb!"

"How else am I goin' to get you out of here?"

"You ain't. You're goin' to get on that horse and get out of here with the Major's money. I'll stay here and keep you covered. I got all the advantage on them."

"They'll come and kill you sure as hell."

"What for? They'll know I ain't got the money. When I've held them long enough for you to get plumb away, they'll know they've lost out. They'll probably get on that horse and head for parts unknown."

Isaac rubbed his sweaty hands against his britches. "I don't like it, leavin' you thisaway."

"You're wastin' time. Damn you, don't try to tell me you ain't wished a hundred times to see me bust a leg; I've seen it in your eyes."

Isaac conceded. "There ain't been a day since you come onto the Big Lonesome that I wouldn't of laughed . . . till now. Now I ain't laughin'."

"You ain't *thinkin'*, either. But I never did see one of you crows that was much on thinkin'."

That did it. Harshly Isaac said, "If that's the way you feel about it, I'll go. But you cover me good. I don't want no bullet in my butt."

"Everything I do, I do good. You just spur that horse."

Isaac untied the rope from the horse's neck and dropped it, making no attempt to retrieve it. The last thing he needed right now was a rope. He swung into the saddle, ducking around the brush as he made his way through the motte. At the back side he took one last look toward Runyan but couldn't see him for the foliage. He shouted, "I'm goin'," and put spurs to the bay.

As he broke into the open and up the slope, Runyan started firing. Isaac heard two or three shots that didn't come from Runyan's rifle, but they were evidently fired in haste and didn't faze him. He kept spurring the bay until he was over the hill. When he looked back and saw he was safe, he drew up on the reins.

The riflefire continued, not all of it Runyan's. Isaac knew his escape had put the two outlaws in a squeeze. If they were to have any chance at the money, they had to break free of Runyan in a hurry. The only way to do that was to run over him.

Isaac sensed from the sound of the shots that they were working closer to Runyan. Runyan had the timber for cover, but he was in no shape to move around. Moreover, the shock and pain of that broken leg were bound to detract from his ability to take care of himself.

They'll run over him, Isaac thought. *They'll flat run over him!*

He pulled the horse to a full stop and turned in the saddle, bracing his right hand on one of the full saddlebags. The feel of it reminded him of his mission, of the necessity of getting the money to the bank before it closed. But that gunfire meant Runyan was in trouble, and it was fixing to get worse.

No skin off of my nose, he told himself. *He's had his spurs into me ever since he come to the outfit. World'd be a damn sight better off it there wasn't no Runyan in it.*

But Isaac could not bring himself to ride on. He cursed himself for his indecision. He pulled the horse around with a violence he would normally have condemned another man for. *Hell's bells, even a Runyan deserves better than this.*

He looked at the tall hill to his right. From up there he ought to have a commanding view of everything below him, of everything west of the motte.

"Come on, you jughead," he said roughly to the horse, socking the spurs to him. "Be damned if they're goin' to kill Runyan. I been savin' that pleasure for myself."

He went up that hill as fast as the horse could climb. A little short of the top he stopped, swung down, and bunched a handful of the tall grass tightly enough that he

162   *Elmer Kelton*

could tie the reins to it. Saddlegun in his hands, he ran
the rest of the way up, his spurs ringing as he tromped
through the grass.

At the top he stopped for a look. He could see down
on the outlaws' one remaining horse, still lying with its
feet tied. But Quain and the other man had crawled
through the grass most of the way to the motte. Isaac
guessed that any moment now they would raise up and
make a run at Runyan. With luck he might get one. He
would not likely get both.

Isaac knelt so he could rest an elbow on his knee as
he took aim, but he found he could not see through the
grass immediately in front of him at that low level. He
had to stand. He spread his feet a little apart to brace
himself, brought the rifle up to his shoulder, drew a deep
breath, and held it. He lined the sights on the man nearest the motte, allowed a little windage, and squeezed the
trigger.

The man jerked and fell backward.

The other one cowered in fear and surprise. Isaac
took a bead on him, squeezed off, and knew he missed.
The man jumped up, throwing his rifle away and raising
his hands. Even at the distance, Isaac knew this was Alvin Quain. Isaac yelled, "Hold him, Runyan. I'm comin'
down."

He turned back, got his horse, and rode down the
hill, back to the motte. He found Quain standing there
a-tremble, his hands still up. Runyan lay just as Isaac had
left him, his back against the tree, his saddlegun trained
on Quain.

Quain began whimpering as soon as Isaac was in
earshot. "Isaac, don't you shoot me! I swear, Isaac, there
wasn't none of this my idea."

Isaac was sorely tempted to shoot him, just for the
pleasure of seeing him jump and fall. But he was getting
sick at his stomach from the shooting that had already
been done.

Quain pleaded. "It was them other fellers. It was
their idea, not mine."

Isaac demanded, "What did you do to the Major?"

"We never done nothin' to him. We didn't even follow him. We figured all along it was you that had the money."

Runyan had guessed correctly. Isaac asked, "Runyan, you all right?"

"Hell yes, I'm all right. Damn you, Isaac, I sent you away. You ain't got the sense of a one-eyed jackrabbit."

Isaac's hands were tight on the rifle. "You ungrateful son-of-a-bitch, I saved your life."

"I could of saved my *own* life; I didn't need you."

Isaac spat, studying Runyan with angry eyes. "If you got to know, I didn't do it for you. I done it for me. If I hadn't come back, I'd of been askin' myself the rest of my life if I was too scared."

Runyan gave him back his angry stare, and Isaac could see resentment. Runyan accused, "Nobody told me you could shoot like that."

"The question never come up."

"Always got to keep tryin' to prove you're the best man, ain't you?"

"I *am* the best man."

Runyan tried to move, but the broken leg brought him sharp pain. "I'm tellin' you one more time to take that money and go to town with it."

"And I'm tellin' you to go to hell; *I'm* in charge of the money. As I climbed that hill I seen a house off down the way. Think if I got you on a horse, you could ride a mile or two?"

Runyan stormed, "Dammit, Isaac, a broken leg ain't fixin' to kill me. Get the Major's money to town like I said. Don't you ever pay any attention to what a white man tells you?"

"*Some* white men." Isaac motioned his rifle at Quain, who had never dared lower his hands. "You pick up that branch yonder and tie it to Runyan's leg so we can keep it straight. Move!"

He held the rifle on the man while Quain splinted Runyan's leg.

That done, and Runyan in a position to keep a gun on Quain, Isaac rode to where the outlaws' remaining horse was tied down. He undid the rope and let the horse to its feet. It wobbled around a minute or so until circulation came back into its legs. Isaac started to leave the rope, then changed his mind and coiled it. He led the horse back to the edge of the motte.

"Quain, you help Runyan get up onto this horse. Hurt him and I'll blow a hole in you that they could run a team of mules through!"

It was a struggle, but Runyan managed to get into the saddle. His face went white, and Isaac knew it would be a lucky thing if Runyan didn't faint dead away. But the cowboy was tough; Isaac had to concede him that.

Isaac shook out a small loop and pitched it over Quain's neck, jerking the slack up tight.

Quain began to cry. "For God's sake, nigger, you wouldn't hang a man."

"For God's sake *what*?"

"For God's sake Isaac. . . ."

Isaac gave the rope a jerk. "You know, I can't remember that in my whole life I ever heard anybody call me *Mister Jefford*."

"For God's sake Mister Jefford!"

Isaac's dry lips parted in a hard grin. He turned to Pete Runyan. "*Mister Jefford.* My, but that does have a nice ring to it. I wonder if I could ever get *you* to call me Mister Jefford?"

Pete Runyan gritted his teeth in pain. "When hell has got ice on it six foot thick."

Isaac shrugged. "Well, sometimes a feller settles for small gains." He dallied the end of his rope around his saddlehorn. "Quain, you'll either keep up or get dragged to death; I don't much care which." To Runyan he said, "I'll get you down to that house where somebody can take care of you, then I'm headin' on to Fort Worth."

They were there in a little while, and a big farmer boy was helping Isaac lift Pete Runyan out of the saddle while the big farmer kept a shotgun trained on a redfaced, panting, rope-burned Alvin Quain. They laid Runyan down on a quilt on the front porch.

Isaac said, "Quick as I get the bankin' business done, I'll send back after you."

As Isaac started to get on his horse, Runyan called him. "I got somethin' to say to you, boy." Isaac turned to listen.

Runyan said, "I ought to've killed you a long time

ago. You got a head as hard as a rock; you won't listen to a damn thing a man tells you. You're uppity, and you got a mean streak in you a yard wide. But I'll give you one thing: you ain't nobody's pet. If there was any way you could bleach that black hide . . ."

Isaac came near smiling, but he didn't do it. "Damn little chance of that, and damn little chance that *you'll* ever change either. Looks like we just got to take each other the way we are."

The bay horse was well used up when Isaac hit town, but he still had a little trot left in him. The shadows of the frame and stone buildings reached more than halfway across the street. Isaac didn't know what the bank's closing time was, but he knew the afternoon was far along. He saw a man walk out of an office which had a sign reading "Attorney." The man closed and locked the door behind him. A sick feeling settled in the pit of Isaac's stomach. If it was so late that an attorney was going home, the bank was probably already shut down. He had often heard people make disparaging remarks about bankers' hours.

Weariness had put a slump in his shoulders, and his eyes were blurry, but doggedly he pushed on up the street. He had not allowed himself even to consider what he could do if he found he was too late. He guessed he could find out from somebody where J. Warren Norris lived and take the money to the banker at his home, but he remembered what the Major always said about Norris being a stickler for the terms of the contract when they were in his favor. Norris could refuse to accept the money if it were offered after he had closed his bank. After all, the loan, strictly speaking, was with the bank, not with Norris as an individual.

Isaac looked longingly toward a saloon, licking dry lips with a tongue that was almost dry itself. He wasn't much of a drinking man, but at a time like this the idea seemed good.

He glanced toward a livery barn and thought how good that hay would feel, just to lie down in it and sleep for two or three days.

He pushed on toward the stone bank. He pulled up

in front of it finally and sat in the saddle, staring. The front doors were closed. His heart sagged.

Too late.

He stared through the glass windows. He blinked the haze from his weary eyes and saw a movement of something white. He blinked again and made out a clerk, wearing a white shirt. The bank might be closed, but someone was still in there. Isaac dragged his right leg across the bay horse's rump, all but falling from the saddle. He braced himself against the horse to keep from going to his knees. When his knees quit trembling he undid the saddlebags, braced himself on the hitchrack a moment, then forced himself up the two steps to the bank's front doors. He tried the knob and found that it turned in his hand. He pushed the door open and dragged himself inside, shutting the door behind him.

The clerk looked up in surprise from a ledger. He stared at Isaac's black face. "You're not our regular sweeper. What're you doing here?"

"I got bankin' business," Isaac said, his voice hardly better than a mumble.

"You'll have to come back tomorrow, boy," the clerk said crisply. "It's after hours."

"The door's still open," Isaac insisted, his voice rising a little, "and I got bankin' business with Mister J. Warren Norris."

"Mister Norris went out awhile ago. You can catch him here in the morning if you have any valid business with him."

"The business I got, I got with him *today*. When's he comin' back?"

"I'll call a constable if you make trouble, boy. I am not one to be trifled with."

"Neither am I," Isaac said stubbornly, thrusting his chin out. "Now, when's he comin' back?"

The clerk quailed a little at the unexpected resistance. "He took a couple of friends for a drink. He was in a jubilant mood over some ranch that defaulted today. If he hadn't left a couple of papers here that need his signature, you wouldn't have found that door unlocked."

Isaac turned, looking for a chair. "But it *was* unlocked, and I'm here, and I'm goin' to wait."

He sat down heavily in a leather-lined chair that had been built strong enough to hold a plowhorse. He stretched his legs out straight in front of him, and he let the saddlebags drop to the floor with a heavy thump.

It was all he could do to keep from nodding off to sleep. To try to stay awake he got to watching the pendulum swing back and forth on a big clock, but that made him drowsier than ever. So he contented himself with watching the clerk, and smiling inwardly over the knowledge that the man was afraid of him. Isaac was sure that if he were not sitting so near the door the clerk would probably dash out into the street to look for a policeman.

He heard laughing voices and footsteps out front. The door hinges protested a little, and he saw the portly figure of J. Warren Norris stride into the bank, followed by two other men in swallowtail coats. Norris was laughing as he turned to close the door.

Isaac pushed himself up from the chair and picked up the saddlebags. "Mister Norris," he said, "I'm Isaac Jefford. I got some business here for Major Lytton."

Very gently he settled the saddlebags on the counter.

ABOUT THE AUTHOR

ELMER KELTON was raised on a West Texas ranch and spent his formative years among cowboys and old-timers. The author of more than thirty novels, Mr. Kelton won his sixth Spur Award from the Western Writers of America in 1994 for *The Far Canyon*. He has won four Western Heritage Awards from the National Cowboy Hall of Fame, the Levi Strauss Golden Saddleman Award for lifetime achievement in Western literature, as well as honors from the Texas Institute of Letters and the Western Literature Association. Mr. Kelton lives in San Angelo, Texas.